I DREAM OF DAMASTION

AN ARMADA WARS ADVENTURE

R. CURTIS VENTURE

ALSO BY THE AUTHOR

In this Series:

Steal from the Devil

List of the Dead

The Ravening Deep

From Shattered Stars

A Storm to the Savage

Whom Gods Shall Fear, Part One

INTRODUCTION

If you're brand new to the Armadaverse, welcome to the party! And a hearty welcome back for those of you who are reading the main sequence novels already.

This novella can be regarded as an expansion episode, telling a story which fleshes out certain aspects of the main storyline of the novels. It describes and expands on events we know must have happened in other places, but which we did not get to 'witness' directly.

You do not need to have read the main sequence novels to grasp the plot of this novella, although it may, of course, be more meaningful if you are aware of the larger universe in which it occurs.

Total newcomers may be confused at first to see [square brackets] used within dialogue. These are explained when they first appear in the text, however I will also give a quick rundown here. Any dialogue in square brackets is called an 'insert', and inserts are used exclusively in speech which has been sampled and duplicated by an alien translation device. The term will most often be a proper noun, or some other idiom or phrase for which there is no equivalent in the alien language.

This story starts at a point towards the end of the third novel, *The Ravening Deep*. It begins during widespread civil unrest across the many worlds, shortly before the culmination of the unsettling strategy which sees the enemy gain a significant strategic advantage in that novel's climax. The action of this novella is spread across about a week, and it therefore also extends into the 'journey time' section at the beginning of the fourth novel, *From Shattered Stars*.

Enjoy!
RCV

1

———

So long, Kementhast. If I said I would miss you I'd be lying.

I have to admit to a certain degree of regret, but that has nothing to do with the planet itself. It's because there was still so much more for me to do down there. Given the present circumstances it does not seem likely that the third stage of my great endeavour will be completed any time soon.

But that is behind me now, quite literally. The mob saw to that.

I suppose I must have known I would need to evacuate eventually. There is only so much civil unrest that can occur before a university will send its students, staff, and visiting academics home, then bar the gates.

It came as something of a surprise, though, to be offered an active, participatory role in the ICS *Ardent*'s unusual mission. A timely surprise indeed — albeit more than a little foreboding — relieving me of the need to make my own way home. As I had become more fully aware of the true extent of the dangers unfolding in the cities, I had also come to learn that getting off-world and heading home would have been far more difficult than I might have reasonably come to expect from past experience alone. For me, of course, past experience is everything, so the confusion and sense of disconnection that I experienced — when I realised I could not simply saunter to the starport and purchase same-day passage — was really quite overwhelming. An unexpected return call from the Navy's local academic liaison officer came just in time to pull me back from a downward spiral of uncertainty and panic.

It had not been long at all before an armoured personnel carrier had arrived, crewed by some very serious-looking men and women with orders to 'extract' me. Despite my growing awareness of the unrest I thought, quite genuinely, that the occupants of this absurdly over-defended vehicle were carrying out some sort of complicated practical joke. Of course the subsequent journey to the starport corrected that naive view.

They let me watch through one of the windows in the side wall of the Kodiak. I say window; it was a long trapezoid of thick glass, more of a protected slit really. The world I saw slicing on by that solid barrier was unrecognisable to me.

The city was upside-down. Sometimes there were people, usually in groups and rarely calm. Those few I saw alone were most often running. A lot of the time the streets were simply empty, but invariably the scars of a mob's wrath were evident wherever I looked. Few windows seemed to have survived intact, and many premises were burned out entirely.

When I did see people actively smashing apart the front of a civic security sub-precinct building, they were frenzied. I've never seen anything quite like that before. The very *raging* of it all. I can't say I have lived here long enough to be intimately, spiritually connected to the mores and leanings of the local populace, not to the degree that I feel as one with them, but I would never have expected that the people living on this world — or indeed on *any* Imperial Combine world — might be capable of descending to destructive tendencies so very quickly.

It still bothers me that I overlooked the warning signs. But then I've been buried in holos for the past few weeks, cloistered away and devoted to a single academic pursuit. And let's be honest here — it's not just me. *Nobody* expects this sort of thing to happen on a world like Kementhast Prime, and why in the many worlds would they?

On a planet like Low Cerin? Oh definitely yes. That little quagmire of a world festers with the dissatisfied, the disaffected, the disenfranchised, and the dispossessed. They say things are so bad there that even the Coalition still holds sway, as anachronistic as that might sound. But here? No. Rebellion is not a recreational activity one would reasonably anticipate. I have walked the streets of this city many times — not so often during this latest visit, admittedly, but still I am certainly no stranger to Kementhast Prime — and the one thing which has always drawn me to stroll, to peruse, to explore a modestly diffused cultural heritage, is this world's ubiquitous, gentle tranquility.

So the degree of contrast has been more than a little unnerving. Even as the Kodiak shouldered its way obstinately through a plaza, creating a passage of its own amongst the citizens and civic security who battled there, it was difficult to accept what was happening right outside that plasteel hull. There were harsh impacts and the scraping of metal on metal, the sounds penetrating the rear cabin of the vehicle in sudden, nerve-wrenching bursts, and still it all seemed like a surreal, immersive street performance.

By the time we reached the starport though, I had seen blood being shed.

There was a short trip on foot from the Kodiak to some sort of military landing craft, and it was during that sprint across the pads that I gained a whole new perspective on matters. Smoke, rising in great billowing columns, congregated in a turgid, brown bank far above the rooftops and spires. Even the noise from the various craft idling on the starport's many pads could not mask the cracks and pops of gunfire behind us.

When you have lived your life working for the betterment of a great civilisation, it is a confusing and bewildering experience to see part of it go up in literal smoke right before your very eyes. Particularly so when it is tearing itself apart from within.

As I reached the ramp at the rear of the landing craft — waved along and hurried verbally by someone I could only assume was crew — I heard a series of sonic booms high in the skies above us. The last thing I saw before I scurried aboard was a group of armoured craft breaking through the clouds and heading for the far side of the city. They were thundering towards the ground as though they really meant business, as if those aboard were eager and determined to deal out yet more damage on the surface of the planet.

Regrettably, thanks to my condition and the tiny implant which augments my control of it, I will never forget any of those scenes. But now I am out of danger. Now I am aboard a brand new navy starship, which seems about as safe a place right now as any in which I could possibly hope to be.

I don't spend a great deal of time gushing over such things, not usually, but I did have to admit that the Imperial Combine Starship *Ardent* was impressively sleek and modern, and — compared to the commercial passenger liners I would usually be obliged to patronise when travelling between star systems — incredibly clean.

They say first impressions count the most, and I am in the unfortunate position of being uniquely qualified to state how absolutely right they are. Remembering everything to which one is ever exposed means that one can measure the accuracy of such a saying with the confidence level of a minor god.

Over time, remaining mindful of that first impression, one gets to know the true difference between who a person is, and who they want others to *believe* they are. There is all too often a large difference between the actual and theoretical personages. I would go as far as to say, in fact, that there is *always* a difference, or to be more precise a set of differences. I call this set of differences the 'personal identification differential'. I score the people I encounter, both for future reference and — I admit it — for my own amusement.

It's fair to say that the ship itself passed all of my 'first impressions' tests, such as they are with regard to inanimate objects. My first impressions of Captain Mansour al-Rashid, as it happens, were also entirely good.

"Welcome aboard the *Ardent*," he said. "On behalf of the Imperial Navy, and her Most Radiant Majesty, I would like to thank you in advance for your time and effort."

"You're too kind, Captain. It still remains to be seen if I will be of any real use to you."

Al-Rashid had stood as I entered — a courtesy I appreciated, old-fashioned as I am — and when he sat down again I noticed that he picked up and toyed with a metal tool I recognised as a letter opener. Antiques like that are a rarity even planet-side, and I wondered exactly who would be sending him letters in this day and age. Presumably he was a man of traditional values, who liked things to be 'real'.

Noted.

He smiled warmly and indicated one of the two chairs before his desk. I stole a look around as I crossed from the door to the chair. His office was just like my study — undeniably lived-in. Yes my study might well be untidy, but I know where everything is. Everything is in its proper place, its *own* place, and convention or tidiness be damned. From the look of his office compartment I suspected the good captain of thinking along the same lines as I.

Thought, now, I suppose, rather than 'thinking'. That was then, and this is now. Whether or not Captain al-Rashid really still *thinks* at the present moment is quite a difficult question to answer. I am certain, however, that when I first encountered him he was still the sole lord and master of more than just his ship.

"You come highly recommended," said al-Rashid. "Three doctorates from two of the top academic institutions in Imperial space, awarded no fewer than four Constellation prizes for—"

"Five," I said. I regretted that at once. "Not to boast, of course."

He smiled at me. "Not at all, you earned them. And I appreciate accuracy — I'm quite sure that accuracy is a condition a physicist will always pursue."

"It most certainly is, Captain."

"Good. My point was, Command feels you are definitely one of the few people most qualified to help shed light on our problem. You will already know, I expect, that you in particular are regarded as one of the finest minds in all the many worlds."

I've never liked accolades, even when they are as well-meaning as this. The problem for me is simple. As well as remembering every individual instance of praise, I also remember every single one of my mistakes — hubristic or otherwise — with a clarity so crystalline it borders on being sarcastic. Congratulations such as these, as an unintended consequence, make me feel like a fraud. An imposter to my own experience, knowledge, and skill. It's not true, of course, but I have always treated myself as though it were.

"It's kind of you to say so," I said. "But Captain, my fear is that your problem might not be fixed simply by applying knowledge or experience or capability. Without the right data it's a multi-variant analysis we're faced with, and sadly we're all wearing blindfolds."

"But that's exactly why you're here," he said. "To identify, capture, and interpret the right data."

"The pre-brief document gave me no clue as to how that might be done."

Captain al-Rashid appeared to stifle a laugh. "Yes, it was rather... brief. Just the problem, not the proposal."

"Am I to assume then that the Navy already has some sort of plan?"

"Now you're safely aboard, I will tell you 'yes'. Or a jumping-off point, at least. We have an idea of what we need to do to get you all started. It just wasn't deemed wise to include any real details in the pre-briefing document, given that we're at war."

"At war?"

There was a very long pause, and I wondered if I should ask again.

"You can't be serious?"

The bewilderment I detected in his voice was genuine — I could see it in his face.

"You'll have to forgive me, Captain. I've been working intensively now for more than a month, in a literal basement. I rarely come up for air when I'm making progress. I've been told I was even ignorant of the unrest on Kementhast for several days."

"So you really don't know what's happening?"

"I *had* heard there were some problems along our borders with Viskr territory, but if I'm honest that wasn't particularly interesting to me."

"Military conflict, rather than just 'problems'. But that was a diversion orchestrated by our true enemy. The entire Imperial Combine is under attack, by a race we've never encountered before."

"Oh," I said.

He seemed disappointed by my reaction, and I can't say I blame him. The fact is that galactic politics barely appear on my radar, and the sabre-rattling of different civilisations' militaries holds no interest for me whatsoever. It's all so primitive.

"Did you not wonder *why* all that was happening on Kementhast Prime?"

"A little," I said. "Although I must admit, since finding out what was going on I've been preoccupied mostly with just getting out of the way. The 'why' of it all hasn't seemed like it should be my greatest priority."

He sighed, and I found myself wondering why he seemed

exasperated. I'd been brought aboard his ship to solve their great navigation problem, not to develop an appreciation for warfare. I can assure you I am no soldier.

"The citizenry across the many worlds has got it into their heads that the Imperial Navy will be abandoning the outer colonies, in the face of an overwhelming invasion."

"I suppose that would explain why they're protesting so vociferously."

"Very much so. It has now been suggested that enemy agents may be provoking matters, to keep us off balance."

"That sounds like it would be a sensible approach."

He eyed me with what appeared to be a mixture of incredulity and suspicion.

"Not that I'm in favour of them using it," I added. "It's just that it's probably very advantageous to them."

"Quite," he said. "As you can imagine, the navigation problem is a hindrance right now. More than a hindrance, in fact — it could cost us the whole war. So believe me when I tell you that the Imperial Combine is willing to do virtually anything to ensure our success."

"And I will certainly do my part," I said.

"You have no idea how glad I am to hear it. We have a quick stopover to make before we get underway properly, then I'll let you know when we're ready to hold the mission briefing for officers and guest specialists. In the meantime, I'll have someone show you to your quarters."

"Before that briefing takes place, Captain, I need to speak with the administration at Kenita-Deng, if it's at all possible. Please. Preferably while we're still in this system."

"I'll see to it that you have comms access from the guest holo in your quarters."

"That would be appreciated, thank you."

"I should warn you though," he said, "your access will be removed quite quickly. Once the mission briefing begins all the general comm access is going to be locked down.

Communications security in this ship is going to be very tight."

That was disappointing, but from what he'd told me by that point I didn't see that even he had any real choice about it.

"An excellent precaution."

"I'm glad you understand." He arose from his chair and extended his hand. "Don't worry, between us we'll have this problem solved in no time. Then you'll be back home before you know it."

I shook the hand he offered. "Nothing could please me more."

"Once again… welcome aboard, Doctor Bel-Kenita."

"Please," I said, "just call me Rex."

Al-Rashid was as good as his word, and before long a crewman of modest rank had shown me to some guest quarters. I was disappointed to find the cabin had no external viewports, but given the volume of the cruiser I should have known better than to expect that any of the best suites would still be vacant. Statistically speaking, the vast majority would be like mine — away from the outer hull, and 'windowless' in the old vernacular.

What the quarters *did* have, however, was a full holo interface — scanner, projector, and all. Strictly speaking I could have sent my message by text only, but it had been a while since I had managed a proper face-to-face discussion with Euelli Berris, and I had told her almost a month ago we would 'talk soon'. Seeing as I was about to leave Imperial territory for a while it seemed rude not to speak with her directly. I dialled in the unified comms address for her offices in the Kenita-Deng station.

The Kenita-Deng factory has orbited Kementhast Prime for almost a century, and it shows. Despite the capital which the company pumps into maintenance and refurbishment, not to mention system refits, it won't be long now before the whole place needs to be decommissioned. I should probably mention that to the board at some point.

Doctor Berris' hologram appeared, then rippled and faded before my eyes. Even their holo transceivers need replacing.

"Rex! I'm glad you got out in time," she said. I had to fill in parts of the words myself, thanks to the signal distortions. "You were starting to worry me."

"You know me well enough. I left it until the last possible moment. The Navy rather forced my hand."

"And a good thing too," she said. "We're now getting reports from the surface that the starport has been overrun. If you'd left it any later you might never have made it off-world."

I don't really have the faintest idea what the mobs on the planet would have done with an academic such as myself, and it is simply not in my nature to worry about unknowns or could-have-happeneds, but for her sake I adopted an expression which I hoped combined satisfactory levels of shock and relief.

"Well… here I am," I said.

"It makes me sad to think about what you're leaving behind," she said. "All that work. Tell me, were you close?"

"Truthfully? Not really. The equations are correct — I'm quite sure of that — but physical application is proving prob-lematic."

"Oh," she said. I could see disappointment written in her face, and with good reason. Kenita-Deng will likely be the first corporation to benefit from my success, if and when it comes, and 'benefit' barely begins to describe how such a success will transform the landscape of the business.

"Silver lining though," I added. "The equations are stored quite safely inside my head. All I've left behind is machinery. You don't need to worry for a single moment about what happens to the labs I was using."

"Oh thank the many worlds," she said. I knew perfectly well she was as concerned for my personal safety as she was for that of my work, even if an outside observer might well question that notion. "You are confident, aren't you? It *will* work?"

"Absolutely. Numbers don't lie, as you know."

"Co-location," she breathed. It was difficult to tell through that low-quality comms channel, but I'm fairly sure her eyes even glazed wistfully. "Imagine it."

"Oh, I have. No more turbulent wormholes, zero transit time, barely any gates needed." I iterated the key benefits of my proposal, somewhat unnecessarily. "The mighty Gate Initiative of yesteryear will seem like a short stroll down a country lane."

"That's putting it mildly," said Berris. "Since the situation on Kementhast has deteriorated so far, the board will of course be very pleased to set you up elsewhere just as soon as you're ready."

"I'm sure they will," I laughed.

She smiled at my reaction, and I had to wonder if she was genuinely pleased for me, or just humouring the man who plans on transforming an empire. I have known Berris for a long, long time, and it could well be the former. She *is* genuinely fond of me. But then I also know how people work, and self-interest is a powerful motivator.

"Anything you need," she added. "A whole new facility if necessary."

"That's most generous," I said. I meant it too.

"I'm sure you understand that Kenita-Deng has considerable interest in your success," she said. "But honestly Rex, *I* want you to succeed. In a thousand Solar years nobody will be interested in who won which Constellation prize. But the man who proved and applied co-location… they'll remember him all right. For a thousand solars and longer, and presumably in galaxies other than this one. Your name will travel as far as humanity's borders."

As much as I appreciated her confidence — and the fact that she answered my unspoken question — I was uncertain how to reply to that. Already in her mind I was a visionary, and she was turning me into the prophet of ages yet to come. Such reverence can be very discomforting to me.

"I'm… it's only because of my implant," I said.

"Nonsense," she sniffed. "That chip can't create anything on its own. It only processes what your own mind passes through it. You can't fool me, Rex. I know you too well."

"But without it I would have been driven mad a long time ago. The information… it's too much. I didn't sleep through a single night until I was augmented."

"So you've said. I can only imagine…"

She trailed off, her face betraying the faintest hint of vicarious agony. She was always empathetic, Doctor Berris. It's one of the reasons I like her so much. That, and her incredible talent for envisioning complex systems. I honestly cannot overstate that talent — if you ever meet Euelli, ask her to show you the 'quadrillion' party trick. She won't mind.

A countdown started in the corner of the screen. I noticed the stars begin to change the direction of their crawl across the view port. *Ardent* appeared to be turning relative to its prior station-keeping, which no doubt meant it was accelerating out of stable orbit.

"Not long left," I told her. "I've been advised that comms will be restricted as soon as the mission briefing is delivered. Official secrets and so forth. You won't be able to reach me."

"You be careful dealing with those Navy people," Berris said. "As civil as they are they're still military. If they want something from you they'll do anything to get it. Don't rely on their smiles."

"That thought had occurred," I said. In all honesty I had not given it much consideration until she prompted me, but the principle is simple enough — people cannot always be trusted. That warning is almost a mantra for me, and I experienced no difficulty in assimilating Euelli's variant of it.

"Good luck, Rex," she said, smiling. "I'm sure you'll ace whatever it is they're hoping you will accomplish."

It didn't take long for me to become bored of the cabin I had been allocated, once that call was over. With nothing to read in preparation for the mission — at least, not until the briefing had taken place and the data packs handed out — I ended up roaming the passageways which had been marked on my holo as unrestricted.

And so I found my way to the mess. As unsociable as I can be sometimes, I think a part of me was yearning for some human contact. Perhaps it was separation anxiety, leaving Kementhast Prime behind as I did when already so far removed from my family. Whatever the reason, it was how I first came to encounter Chief Turei.

Within mere minutes of my own arrival she had sat directly opposite me. She must have seen some surprised micro-expression escaping from my deliberately impassive face, because she laughed out loud immediately and said—

"I can go elsewhere if you'd like? If I'm bothering you?"

That was by no means too much awkwardness for me to bear, but it was slightly more of it than I had bargained for so soon after sitting down to eat my... whatever it was. I took my time chewing and swallowing before I replied, to make sure I didn't say completely the wrong thing. Spontaneity rarely works out well for me, and so I often tend to think then speak.

"It's fine, really. I think I actually wanted to be bothered."

"You know," she said, while establishing herself firmly in the contoured seat, "we *are* going to be seeing a lot of each other anyway, so we might as well make a start now."

"We are?"

"Absolutely. I'm chief snipe. I don't need to ask who *you* are, some of us geeked out a little when we were told you were coming."

"Snipe?"

"Sorry, engineer. You've never heard that name being used?"

"I usually travel on commercial craft. I'm not really familiar with all the naval terminology."

"Oh, okay. This could be fun."

So that's how we met. Zana Turei, that was her name.

Even if I didn't have my particular condition, I thought at the time, *I would still be remembering* you, *that's for sure.*

Surprisingly, I spent far longer eating and talking than I had expected I would even as I had sought out a companion.

The chief engineer covered her mouth with the back of her hand every time she laughed. I don't think it was conscious, and so I also don't think it was meant to be cute, but that's how it seemed to me. I found that a little intriguing, because it's not often I find other people to be cute. 'Cute' is not even a word I generally find much use for in daily life.

"What did I say now?" I asked.

"You said 'floor'," Zana chuckled. "Aboard ship it's always called the deck."

"The deck," I said. The vocabulary item was stored. Truth be told I've heard the term used aboard ships a lot, I just never thought it actually mattered.

"Walls are bulkheads, corridors are passageways, ceilings are the overhead."

"Simple enough."

"Doors are hatches, any sort of room or cabin is a compartment. And nobody is *on* the ship — we're all *in* it."

"I've been sounding like a real tourist, haven't I?"

She replied by way of a smile, and spooned more food into her mouth.

"I just don't fly that often," I said, "and when I do I spend a lot of the travel time reading."

She swallowed. "Honestly, don't worry about it. A lot of people let that last one in particular slide without bothering to correct it — it's more ancient tradition than anything. Virtually all civvies get this stuff wrong, anyway. Nobody uses the right lingo on passenger liners."

"*In* the ship makes a lot more sense," I said. "Travelling *on* the ship would be less than optimal."

"It certainly would," she said.

There was a quiet moment in which it appeared she had decided to shelve our conversation while making some actual progress on her portion of the barely identifiable food available in the crew mess. Not wishing to be rude — but also because I had run out of awkward patter as quickly as I had finished off my own meal — I didn't interrupt.

The mess was busy. I had no idea why at the time, but it did occur to me later that I'd seen some people eating what I might consider to be breakfast foods, while others ate what appeared to be evening meals. Picking those details out of memory tripped an automatic 'compare and contrast: analysis' routine, and I concluded that different shifts must be crossing over. Some people in a starship had to be awake while others slept, after all, ergo the timetables of their daily cycles intersected in different places.

And then I looked again and she was staring at me, and all her alleged food was gone.

"So what is it like?"

I knew exactly what she meant, even as I gave her my stock response of feigned innocence.

"What do you mean?"

Inside I wanted to die a little. It was the same conversational moment I've heard a thousand times before (actually one hundred twenty-nine times, my implant's metadata node informs me), and I will hear it many thousands of times again. It puts me off speaking to people. I mean if they're genuinely curious about it then that's fine. But if they are conspicuously not *so* curious as to do a little research first — to ensure that they don't cause upset or offence — then they're probably not my kind of people. That observation is just one particular quirk that has been shaken out of my automatic, statistical analysis of the demographics I've been exposed to.

The point is, though, that I knew exactly what she was about to say.

"Having an eidetic memory," she said.

She looked amazed and confused as she realised I had mouthed the exact words along with her.

"I don't," I said. "That's just gossip. From people who can't remember an even bigger word than that."

After a slight moment of hesitation she smiled. "Try me."

"Hyperthymesia," I said. "But it's me, so not just *any* old form of hyperthymesia, oh no. I have managed to be affected by an aggressive variant, one called branched-association hyperthymesia."

"I have no idea what any of that means," she said.

"No, very few people do."

I'm never sure if I want to tell others about this. Not just because it's sort of a vulnerability — and who likes to reveal those to total strangers — but also because most well-meaning individuals immediately start to treat you like you have special needs in all things, or like you can't think for yourself all of a sudden, or need help with basic daily tasks or routine choices. So many of my conversations, additionally, have been killed stone dead by a phrase such as "oh, have you considered trying such-and-such…"

She seemed both bright and inquisitive, however, and I was conscious we would likely be working together for some time, as she had herself suggested. So it was obvious that the matter absolutely would come up again at some point.

I might as well get ahead of it, I thought.

"To keep it simple, you can think of hyperthymesia as being a fundamental inability to forget anything."

"Wow—" her response began.

The probability table contained in the data node of my implant is extremely clear on how the structure of this particular conversation will unfold. The likelihoods involved are very strongly skewed. So it was not without good reason that

I opened my mouth at the same time as her, and again recited what I was certain her next words would be:

"Ooh, I'd *love* to be able to remember absolutely *everything!*"

She looked as confused as I must have done when I realised that she was actually saying completely different words altogether, and I had to shuttle back a second or two into active memory to hear what she had actually said.

"—that sounds like an unmitigated nightmare."

I didn't need to consult any data storage node of my augmentation to know that that was the first time I have ever had that response, or even one remotely like it. In the interests of being accurate I have since checked, but I needn't have done so.

She must have become impatient waiting for me to reply. "Is it? I bet it is."

"You have no idea," I said. "And to be honest I'm a little taken aback that you even thought that. Most people seem to think that me describing it as a disability is some kind of infinitely ungrateful crime against nature."

"Yeah," she said. "But then most people don't seem to know they're supposed to *think* during a conversation."

It was at that exact point that I knew I really, genuinely liked Zana. That doesn't happen to me very often.

2

____

W ah-a-la-han Anchorage is, so I have been told, the most remote human-controlled facility on the downstream Orion arm of our galaxy. I say human-controlled, rather than just 'human', because as its name suggests the station was built and established by others, and used by them prior to our current period of occupancy.

Nobody knows what happened to the Wah-u-laki species. If my disappointingly brief enquiries with the shipboard database were anything to go by, nobody seems to care very much either. I find that more than a little curious, because one of the details that is very well-recorded is how absolutely pristine their ruins are. They're not even really ruins; if the descriptions are to be believed they are more like very dusty, vacant premises, empty of life but not of the evidence that life was once there. It is said to be as though the entire population of a multi-world civilisation simply got up and left one day, abandoning everything from their planet-side cities to space facilities like the anchorage. I would have thought people would want to get to the bottom of that, but apparently not.

I located the initial account of the first discovery of these worlds — written by the ex-military, self-styled explorer Captain Kierton — but he was never particularly studious when it came to the actual archaeological science of detailing and explaining his various findings. The only other really scholarly effort came from the journals of Helbrunt Bel-Undosa, published by his presumed widow long after his own disappearance and the subsequent discovery of his empty exploration craft and abandoned research camp.

Now I'm no xeno-historian, nor am I an exo-archaeologist, but I find these mysteries very intriguing. Were I in either of those career paths I probably would not rest until I knew what happened — to both the Wah-u-laki, and to those who vanished while trying to solve that earlier riddle. Other than limited surveys conducted by under-funded academics, there appear to be no more actions being taken to tell us why, or even *how*, a whole sentient species went missing so suddenly and so completely. I suppose that was inevitable, now that a new superstition has arisen; those people best positioned to solve the puzzle are afraid of disappearing themselves.

Yet there we were using the possibly cursed anchorage for our own space-faring purposes. Waste not want not, I suppose. I mean it did the job, and there were certainly no Wah-u-laki around to object. To my knowledge nobody stationed at Wah-a-la-han anchorage has vanished since the Imperial Navy occupied it.

Perhaps the spirits of the Wah-u-laki are pleased with our motives, and they shield us from the night.

I should probably take a moment just now to explain precisely where Wah-a-la-han is. It occurs to me that this detailed record of mine may well end up with someone who lacks any great knowledge of galactic cartography, and it's important to understand just how far we were already — even right at the start of our mission — from anything and everything that generally matters to our people. After all, I am likely to be the last survivor of our current situation, and with the circumstances as they are nobody else, *nobody*, can be relied upon to create an accurate and honest account of our particular catastrophe.

Let's start with the same convention that every Imperial Combine schoolchild is taught. Imagine the view of the galaxy from 'above', such that the rotation of the great spiral arms is clockwise around the galactic core. Now find the Orion arm — it's neither in the central mass of the inner core, nor is it out at the galaxy's edge. It's a relatively short spiral arm, squashed up in the middle of the galaxy's disc. Our home star, Sol, is about one quarter of the way down that, measuring from Orion's leading edge. Keep moving down the Orion arm, against the rotation of the galaxy, and after travelling two thirds of that arm's length you'll find my home, Damastion, orbiting the star Axicon as quietly and serenely as ever she has.

When you arrive at that planetary system, they say, you've reached the limit of real civilisation on the Orion arm. But to get to Wah-a-la-han you must keep going.

The Orion arm is sort of lucky, in a way. On either side of most arms of the galaxy lie the Deep Shadows, huge gulfs of low stellar density. Orion arm though is cosseted, sandwiched snugly between the Sagittarius, Perseus, and Carina arms. There are small areas of Deep Shadows on either side of us, sure, but those regions are relatively narrow when compared to the silent, brooding oceans bordering some of the greater spiral arms. The Orion arm is overlooked by many neighbours, rather than being surrounded by the terrorising, soundless scream that is the dark wilderness.

Until you reach the terminus systems of Orion's Reach, that is. When you arrive at that trailing edge of Orion, far downstream, you are among straggler stars, those which seem to chivvy and chide along their planet-brood as if afraid they will all be left behind. You are looking straight out into a gulf that stretches on for thousands and thousands of near-sunless light years before encountering at last the outermost arm of the galaxy. Even out-of-system, away from atmospheres and gravity wells and the showy glare of planets and local stars, the view looking into that region is wrong somehow. If you expected a glorious firmament to glisten back at you, you would feel short-changed. It is infused with an eerie, chilly sort of emptiness, and it can stare back at you for far, far longer than you can possibly bear to squint fearfully into it.

And that's where you'll find Wah-a-la-han, and all the other silent, abandoned worlds that were once occupied by the Wah-u-laki people. That's where the anchorage was, still is, and that's where the *Ardent* was compelled to stop and top up supplies before beginning the mission proper. Right at the end of human space.

It was where matters first turned against us, not that we knew it at the time.

It had not escaped my notice that in order to reach the tail end of Orion, coming as we had directly from Kementhast Prime, the *Ardent* had had to pass by Damastion. Okay, perhaps 'pass by' is something of an exaggeration — given that the closest we came to my beloved home was two-hundred or so light years, and we were in wormhole transit at the time — but I would be lying if I said the silliness of it did not affect me.

It's fine, I ended up telling myself. *The goal does not have to be to get home as quickly as possible, with the smallest distance travelled — it is enough simply to get home. This ridiculously long diversion is part of the price, which I agreed to willingly.*

And so to demonstrate to myself how seriously I took my obligations to Captain al-Rashid, and to the Imperial Combine Navy, I linked to Chief Engineer Turei and offered my assistance.

"Sure," she said. "I'm only going to be directing the on-boarding of our supplies, but by all means come and help. It will probably be fairly educational for you, if nothing else."

By the time I reached main engineering the *Ardent* had docked physically with the anchorage. Most of Zana's work crews had left the engineering compartments already, headed for the port-side cargo holds. Zana had stayed behind to wait for me.

Her smile was slightly strained — just enough to notice, but I think maybe not so much that most people would — and I wondered if that was on my account.

"Sorry," I said. "Have I made you wait?"

"It's fine. I'm usually there right from the start, but I guess my people know well enough what they're doing. Let's get going."

We hurried back the way I had come, out of main engineering and into the passageways of the ship. But where I had approached from one direction at the first junction, we now used the opening for the opposing route.

"Is this a normal activity for you? For your ship, I mean," I said. She walked very briskly and I had to trot slightly to keep up, every fifth step or so. "I've never experienced something like this on commercial flights."

"You wouldn't," she said. "The shipping companies don't want passenger liners waiting idle. They're being serviced by shuttles and other utility craft the moment they start to approach orbital facilities."

"They keep them in motion."

"Exactly," she said. "Before the umbilicus even connects, baggage, cargo, and effluent has been off-loaded and fresh resources pumped in. By the time you've alighted from the aft locks, hygiene fields are sweeping from prow to stern, the flight crew has been rotated, a 'bot has started brewing coffee, and a new set of passengers is boarding at the forward locks. It's a smooth operation that keeps running costs way down."

"But you— we don't have that concern?"

"Nope," she said. "We take the time to do it right and then check everything four or five times over. It saves having an avoidable disaster at exactly the wrong moment."

"I get it," I said. "And so hard-docking makes sense, because we might be here a while."

"Yeah. We always hard-dock with an anchorage. We can stretch our legs in a more coherent gravity field. We can actually speak with the quartermaster, see what special somethings she can rustle up for us. And of course, cargo transfer is far safer."

We rounded a corner and had to step to one side, avoiding a crew member who was mopping the deck. That too was something I had never seen on a commercial flight. In fact, checking my records quickly, I don't have any memory of ever seeing a human actually pushing a mop around, and I only know what that particular tool is because as a teen I saw it referred to in a history multimedia package.

"Chief," the crewman said as we passed by. He looked our way but kept his head down.

Zana nodded silently, and we rounded the next corner.

"Do navy vessels not use hygiene fields?" I said.

"Of course. They're standard fit."

"So why was he…?"

"Ha," she said. "Mister Cona is on jankers."

"Jankers?"

"Punishment detail — learned that one from infantry, and it seems to work well. Do you mind if we take this ladder down a couple of decks? I'm not going forward three sections just to use an elevator and then come all the way back again."

"Sure. Punishment for what?"

"Cona was responsible for setting up a still I found yesterday. Vodka, I think. So I've made him the *Ardent*'s floor king. He's swabbing that passageway until I say he's done."

"It was a very short passageway."

"Yeah, but like I said — until *I* say he's done. He's been going back and forth since the commencement of this duty shift."

"Is that a good use of resources?"

"In a way," she said. "I mean obviously other people have to compensate for his absence in engineering, but what you have to remember is that his still is the only one I've found. I'd like all the other idiots who've set up potentially explosive distilleries in my ship to reconsider their actions."

"Good point," I said. "I had no idea things like this even went on."

"Why would you?" She said. "Welcome to the navy life. Don't worry, with your abilities I'll have you up to speed in no time."

I wondered as we walked and talked how it was that Zana — devoid as she was of augmentation — could remember all the lefts and rights and downs that we had to take to reach the cargo holds. But we got there in the end, and not once did she refer to a printwall for directions, so I came to the conclusion that Chief Zana Turei must have known the passageways of *Ardent* inside-out.

I should be clear that that was no mean feat. As far as I am aware the *Ardent* was the prototype and sole example of the brand new Avignon-class design. Granted Zana had probably first come aboard when the cruiser was still under construction in the Noroconte shipyards — the very moment life support was brought online in the engineering sections, I suspected — but it could not have been more than a couple of months before this first mission began, and she would not have been able to walk the passageways constantly.

Perhaps not surprisingly the cargo holds were the least impressive part of the ship I had seen so far. Large boxes, essentially. Spaces carved out of the ship, several decks in height, which were devoted almost entirely to storage. Cargo-scale airlocks provided access from the port side of the ship to the rigid space bridges which connected our cruiser to the anchorage. I could see the inside of standard lock fittings at our end, but how the bridges interfaced with the alien architecture of the anchorage I couldn't say. I suppose someone like the empire's Engineering Corps must have solved that problem a long time ago, because the bridges — spaced out and aligned according to the specifications for large-frame naval vessels — were clearly permanent, fixed structures, bearing many clear signs of use.

Zana spent a few minutes conversing with deck hands

and members of her engineering teams, directing them in a broad fashion to make the best use of the available space. I was just starting to lose interest when she turned to me suddenly and jerked her head towards the nearest lock.

"Let's go," she said. "Quartermaster isn't going to harass herself."

We walked through both the inner and outer hatches of the fully open airlock — an unsettling experience, since in every airlock I have ever traversed the cardinal rule is that only one hatch can be open at any given time — and emerged into the space bridge. The discomfort of walking through a basically disabled airlock faded quickly, such was the design of the bridge. In terms of interior structure it was exactly like any generic passageway aboard ship. You would not have known that just a few centimetres away, literally on the other side of every bulkhead, was not a cosy compartment or another safe passageway, but raw vacuum and the searing radiation of the local sun. Even gravity plating had been installed, although this was more likely to do with moving cargo about safely rather than making passengers feel comfortable.

Inside the anchorage, of course, things became much less familiar very quickly indeed. Zana seemed to know where she was going, and I had no clue myself, so I simply followed her lead. The bridges opened out into a cavernous storage hangar, criss-crossed with racking within which automated, run-on-rails 'bots whizzed up and down, left and right, back and forth, presumably retrieving parts and supplies for the docked *Ardent*. Men and women drove around the space in open buggies, collecting consignments from the 'bots, and then zipped the items over to an area where crates were being loaded. I wondered idly why different 'bots could not perform that undemanding task. Probably because they aren't unionised, I told myself with an inward smile.

Someone yelled something at us about hardhats, but Zana

just grinned and waved. She ushered me towards the leftmost bulkhead and the first major opening within it.

"Not putting on a hard hat just to take it off again," she said. "This passageway will take us to the QM. If there's anything physics-y you think you might need on this trip, you should try and requisition it here."

"Physics-y?" I said. "I thought you were a fan."

She smiled coyly. "Fine, fine, any serious instrumentation or very precise measuring devices."

"Now you're talking my language," I said.

"Oh," Zana said. "Wow, I had no idea…"

I saw she was staring straight ahead and so I too looked where she was looking. At the other end of the passageway, coming in our direction, I saw a human crew member walking patiently alongside a man-sized worm creature.

"Lem Bataan?" I said.

"Yeah," said Zana. "I didn't know any were coming on this mission. You ever met one?"

"Never," I said. "I mean I know about them, of course, but I've never had the opportunity to meet one. Or even be in the same room."

The Lem Bataan and its escort approached. I saw from the woman's rank insignia that she was a commander, the *Ardent*'s executive officer in fact. Even as I picked out this detail she slowed to a stop, and then she actually performed the smallest of bows to Zana and me. I guess she must have been reminding herself all shift not to offend the Lem Bataan she was due to welcome aboard, and just got a bit carried away with rehearsing the diplomatic niceties.

"Mol Gai," she said, "may I present our chief engineer aboard the *Ardent*, Zana Turei."

"I'm honoured to meet you," said Zana.

The Lem Bataan made its own sibilant vocalisations, and a pendant device blinked rapidly. The delay before the audio translation began was almost non-existent.

"The honour is mine, [Zana Turei]. To be invited to join

such an interesting scientific venture, out into the endless dark."

Something caught my attention about the translation pendant's pronunciation of Zana's name, and I played back Mol Gai's words in my active memory. Yes, it was indeed as I thought; the device had actually copied and clipped the commander's pronunciation of Zana's name, in real time, and played that audio back to us embedded correctly in its own synthesised translation.

What a marvellous machine, I thought. No doubt it had been physically built by the Lommu-Bata — a co-evolved, companion race of the Lem Bataan — but it was likely conceived, planned, and ultimately designed by Lem Bataan minds.

"You are *the* Mol Gai, then?" Said Zana. "The gravity guru? Man, I never thought I'd be meeting him. Her. Him?"

"In the most formal settings I am Mol Gai uwul Tah Oss Droum," it said. "Mol Gai is sufficient. I had heard of that nickname your people sometimes use for me. The study of gravity is indeed my passion. And to prevent any uncomfortable misunderstandings you may, for the duration of our expedition, consider me to be male. I have no plans to express otherwise for the time being."

"Thank you for your kind consideration," Zana said. She hit my elbow with her own.

"Thank you for your kind consideration," I echoed, hoping that I sounded sincere. Truth be told that conversation had left me behind very quickly indeed. Express what now?

The Lem Bataan turned to face me. The features I presumed to be sensory organs were small and underformed, as one might expect from an evolutionary route which had in one age passed through the domain of annelid-like organisms, and I quickly discerned that Mol Gai used external apparatus to help him see and hear, as well as to translate. Even his breathing was augmented, with a series of tubules delivering supplementary gasses into the open spiracles in his flanks. The system made a distinctive *hiss-click, hiss-click* sound, and I was suddenly struck by the notion that Mol Gai was self-evidently reliant on devices even more so than I.

"And this," said the commander, "this is..."

She drew out the last syllable and continued to wave her hand slowly in my direction. A large part of me wanted to see what she would do if I simply left her hanging, but something told me I would regret that later on.

"Reximillian Bel-Kenita," I said. "Physicist. I too was invited to join the scientific venture."

"You are the human who knows wormholes," said Mol Gai. "Yes, I have learned of your work."

I looked from Zana to the commander — who, I noted, had been diligent in trying to introduce everyone except for herself — as if either of them might provide clarification. Why in the many worlds would a Lem Bataan know of my work? And why imply that nobody else in the Imperial Combine understands wormholes properly? I know I can be modest, but even so I had no idea my papers had been read so widely that they had reached Lem Bataan space, or that they were held in such high regard there.

"I'm flattered that you have heard of me, Mol Gai," I said. "But what do you mean, I am 'the human'—"

"I hate to interrupt," said the commander. "But there *will* be an informal mixer for crew and guest specialists, straight after the mission briefing. Before that I really must get Mol Gai to sickbay, with enough time to ensure his recent vaccination package has taken effect. Standard procedure and all that."

"Of course, Commander," said Zana.

"We will talk soon, [Reximillian Bel-Kenita]," said Mol Gai.

After they had left us and resumed their trip up the passageway — Mol Gai moving with an undulating, sinusoidal motion, and the commander walking more slowly than she surely would on any other day — I turned immediately to Zana.

"What in the Deep was that about?" I said.

"The bit about you? How should I know? Maybe the *Soor-Ais* have you under surveillance."

"Sore rays?" I said. "What are those?"

"No, *Soor-Ais*. The Lem Bataan secret intelligence service, which officially speaking we definitely don't know about."

"Oh, I see. I think. And you say they could be watching me?"

"I did say it as a joke. But then I suppose it depends on what you've been doing."

The rest of our short trip through the passageways of the anchorage passed without incident, and it was not long before we were in the storefront-style offices of the quartermaster. I got the sense she and Zana were acquainted already, though not from meeting here. It was clear they had accumulated some history in another time and place, but neither of them seemed particularly eager to explain it. And why should they?

"Sappaas ya'll ba waanting whatava fraabies ya can gaat," the quartermaster said. "Lamma chack what's aan ma laast."

The Dunneselorian accent has always confused and disoriented me. It emerged in the Herses system, some considerable time *after* Ramm Stallahad was first settled, colonised, and civilised. It has never been clear to me why the colonies established on Dunneselori ended up extending most of the vowel-based phonemes in their speech. None of their neighbours did that, and it makes me uncomfortable when so many people do things which to me seem so purposeless.

Recalling the quartermaster's words is actually fairly discomforting. I'm going to have to adjust these memories on the fly, otherwise I will end up fire-walling them out of sheer frustration. As much as I think the QM can speak with whatever accent she likes, inside *my* head I'm the boss and it's my sense of propriety I care about most.

"Suppose you'll be wanting whatever freebies you can get," the quartermaster said. "Lemme check what's on my list."

That's much better.

"We must be ruining your day," said Zana. "Coming in here barely announced and taking all your supplies."

"Nah," said the QM. She tapped at her holo. "Your standard supply layout has barely been touched since your launch from the shipyards. No great bother to me."

"Why are we here then?" I said.

Both Zana and the quartermaster looked at me as though I didn't know anything at all, then Zana turned to the QM.

"Yes, he's a landlubber," she said. Then she turned back to me. "Standard operating procedure. We could be under-provisioned by just one packet of dry biscuits, but going out into the Deep we will *always* stop off first and provision to exact specifications."

"Yeah. You don't want to get stranded in the endless void without enough biscuits," said the quartermaster. "Let's see — we're topping you up in twenty-one food categories, and bolstering your stock of spare parts by almost a whole per cent. Filling your water tanks back up to the top line as well."

"Good," said Zana. "Always hated the thought of recycled. If I know we have a full tank I can keep telling myself it's the first pass."

"With water it's never the first pass," I said. "It's all been getting recycled for billions of years."

"True," the quartermaster said. "But my girl here is talking about chemical and mechanical recycling. Water that gets transpired out of plants is just water. Water that cycles through the veins of a cruiser like yours is basically dilute urine."

It took me a moment to compress and inflect all the vowels in that properly, and when I did I screwed up my face involuntarily. That's an unusual reaction for me — I'm usually quite good at controlling the emotions I give away to people. But the idea of bathing in dilute urine, the idea of *drinking* it...

Zana smirked at me.

"I do have a surplus of hydration pouches shown in storage," said the quartermaster. "As well as a whole bunch of magnetic scanners and whatnot. Requisitioned for an expedition to some of the Wah-u-laki worlds. Never went ahead in the end, and the organisers decided to vanish instead of paying up."

"What'll that cost me?" Zana said. "Navy isn't too hot on paying for things it can claim it already provides."

The quartermaster was about to answer, but my determination not to drink urine got the best of me. I am fairly well off. I didn't need to wait while two people who knew each other's manoeuvres bargained and haggled.

"I'll get it," I said. "The water that is — we can share it. Unless you need any of the other equipment?"

"I've got the full list here," said the QM. She flicked data from her holo to Zana's.

"You'd really pay for all that? For both of us?"

"To not drink urine?" I said. "Absolutely."

3

———————

"Thank you all for coming," said Captain al-Rashid.

I'm sure I couldn't have been the only person who found that slightly redundant — half the people in the wardroom were members of his crew, obligated to be there by their duties, and the other half were being well-compensated in one fashion or another. But courtesy is never a waste of time, I suppose.

"Now that we're under way from Wah-a-la-han, and there's no chance of information leaking off-ship, I can provide you with significantly more details about the mission we are all undertaking. I appreciate that many of you will have agreed to take part in this effort with basically no clue what will be required of you, and I thank you for your patience. The first thing I would like to assure you of is that this mission has an extremely low risk profile. We will not be anywhere near the theatre of combat. Far, far from it, in fact."

For reasons I can't explain that particular hazard wasn't something that had yet occurred to me, but it had clearly occurred to others. A ripple of relief passed around the compartment, as if half the occupants had been holding their breath.

"Commander Ouellet," al-Rashid said. "Can you confirm comms lockdown, please?"

His executive officer tapped her holo for a moment. "Confirmation received from the command deck. Comms are secure. Nothing is leaking off-ship from this point onwards."

"Thank you," said al-Rashid. He straightened himself up and squared his shoulders. "The remainder of this briefing should be considered classified. As some of you may know already, the Imperial Navy is experiencing a serious issue with our wormholes. In fact so are a lot of ships and gates in our space, not just those operated by the navy.

"We don't know whether it's flaws in our navigational software, problems with our gravity needle generators, an unknown cosmic phenomenon, or some fundamental misunderstanding of wormhole physics that is just now beginning to become apparent. What we *do* know is that the issue affects the accuracy of wormhole projection, and it's getting worse and worse as time goes by.

"Everyone who has been asked to join us — to complement the experience and skills of our own scientists and engineers — has been chosen because they are a clear leader in a related field. Commander Ouellet."

Al-Rashid took a step back, and Ouellet took his place. She thumbed the base of a holo ring at the head of the wardroom table, and a glimmering, volumetric representation of our galaxy appeared directly in front of her. The map slid inwards and rotated until it showed the ship's specific position.

"The *Ardent* is, as you have probably heard by now, an advanced prototype. Every system uses cutting edge technology, and that includes our conventional engines, our reactor core, and our GNG coils. They're all the latest versions, based on revised models which have been tested over billions of cycles in simulated spaces. The specific units actually fitted aboard this ship have of course all been factory calibrated. Assuming what we know about wormhole technology is accurate, this ship represents the absolute pinnacle of what humanity can currently build.

"Our mission is a game of two halves. Firstly, we will take the *Ardent* on a trajectory away from the plane of galactic rotation, paralleling the Deep Shadows downstream of Orion and putting as much void around us as possible. That will reduce the chances of us suffering enmeshment as we jump in and out of wormholes, over and over. It should also allow us to measure our actual, real-world GNG output functions, to a degree of precision which would usually be prevented by the background noise of intersecting gravity wells."

This prompted what sounded to me like a murmur of excitement from one side of the room, and I gathered that some of my fellow physicists' ears had pricked up at the news that we would, for all practical intents and purposes, be heading out of the galaxy. I gathered they were getting carried away with notions of conducting experiments of their own while they had such a unique opportunity.

"Secondly, we will be taking suggestions for any experimental methods to duplicate or mitigate the nav issues we have been seeing. Nothing will be considered too out there. If you think you might be onto something you let either me or your team leader know, and by all the many worlds we'll get your hypothesis tested."

I could see from the nonchalant reactions to that last bit of information that most of the scientists and engineers present — which as far as I was concerned was anyone not in a naval uniform — had worked out during the briefing that that was how they would be spending their time aboard the *Ardent*.

They, of course, had likely been following the development of this navigation problem as reports came in from across an entire empire. I felt somewhat left behind, having missed quite a lot of daily news while working on my passion project, and I resolved to get myself up to the same speed as the rest of the Imperial Combine's intelligentsia at the first opportunity. In my mind, I pinned a small note to the topmost strip of my field of vision.

Al-Rashid had taken over again.

"I realise a lot of you will want to know exactly how long you will be away from your own work and your families. It would be good to work on this for as long as we need to, but the Navy has agreed a cap of four Solar weeks. That's so as not to inconvenience you to an unreasonable degree.

"Now we've made a stop at the anchorage we are extremely well-provisioned. Our machining bays also have full stocks of all the usual parts, tools, and devices we can't fabricate from scratch. With all of you aboard as well, we could not be better equipped to tackle this problem. Go team!"

There was an uncomfortably long moment of hesitation before one or two of the navy officers led a few of the guests in a self-consciously anaemic round of applause. I felt bad for al-Rashid — he had tried to show his enthusiasm for the mission, and for his dedication to working so closely with civilians, and it had fallen very flat. From his expression though it did not seem to deflate him.

"A final word from me," said al-Rashid, "and then I'll let you all go and get ready for this evening's reception. As you heard prior to the briefing, general access to comms is now prohibited. All requests for off-ship communications must come through my command team. Please do not attempt to bypass that procedure. That's the last thing I need to tell you, so I'll leave you in the capable hands of my XO. Thank you, everyone."

The briefing drifted apart from itself, with Commander Ouellet remaining up front to speak about the data packs she had had prepared for us (those ship's procedures and protocols from which we couldn't simply abstain, the known technical and physical details of the navigation issues, and the structures of the teams in which we would be working). I added more notes into my field of vision and went to accept my pack.

The next few days were very busy for everyone, but I in particular had a great deal of reading and reviewing to get on with. Fortunately I was more than up to the task. Being able to remember what you see and hear extremely accurately on the first pass is exactly the benefit most people imagine it would be. It's the other side of my condition that's the problem, the bit people know nothing about and would disregard if they were told of it. You probably don't want to know the details of that part though.

Yes, the advantages of hyperthymesia are often difficult to deny. For example, it did not take me long at all to get myself up to speed in the periods of downtime available to me. I spent the first few days of our voyage rising half an hour earlier than I really needed to, sacrificing a small amount of sleep so that I could educate myself. I took a holo wherever I went and was diligent in spending my free time reading from it. I sought out the people best positioned to fill in any gaps in my knowledge. Everything I placed in front of myself to study, or was told by another, I retained. It could not have happened any other way, of course.

While I was at it, I took the time to read what humanity had learned and analysed with regard to the Lem Bataan, in the time which had elapsed since the clinic tried to educate me as a pre-implant child. The most fascinating aspect was indeed the concept of 'expressing' — I had been taught in my youth that Lem Bataan genders were not like our own. Nowadays, it would seem, we know better. Our allies can change their gender at will, from male to female or vice versa, but they have learned that humans are generally less confused and uncertain if individuals 'express' one gender or the other consistently during periods of cooperation and social exposure.

I don't think they should have to do that, personally, but I am acutely aware that with my condition I am able to track changes in such details as another being's identity with ease. I suppose other people, with their sponge-like memories, their limited capacity for moving information reliably between working memory and long term storage, and their laughable attention spans, will find it far more difficult. I suppose also that the Lem Bataan know what they're doing in adopting this polite behavioural policy — they did, after all, devise it for themselves.

The bulk of my study time, however, was of course spent on catching up with the rest of the scientists who have been drafted in to help. The problem facing the Imperial Combine was, I learned, on the face of it very simple. The destination apertures of wormholes had started to become less accurate, the problem was getting worse with time, and nobody could yet explain either of those things.

I'm sure I don't need to tell you that solutions are more difficult than problems. Everybody says 'knowing the problem is half of the battle'. What they fail to mention is that the *other* half of the battle is usually far more trying, and it sometimes includes weeping or maybe even a free bloodbath. After speaking to Zana, her engineering teams, and many of the scientists also trying to help explain and fix the issue, I discovered that the whole endeavour was indeed infused with a great deal of shared frustration.

Mol Gai in particular was clearly coming to his wits' end with understanding the problem. I came to know him fairly well in a short space of time — working as we did from the same compartment, one of many the crew had made fully available to their civilian guests. Even taking into account the gulf of our linguistic and cultural differences, his bafflement at the puzzle before us was clear. I could even tell that to some degree he actually blamed himself for not being able to see the cause of the wormhole issue, as though the insufficiency of his insight in this one case somehow made his expertise useless and him solely responsible.

"The gravity needle generator is operating the way it

should, [Rex]," he said, half way through one duty shift. "I am confident in the diagnostic results. The specifications are also very clear — these GNGs are the best the Imperial Combine has ever manufactured."

"Then why are we still seeing a growing error margin?" I said.

Mol Gai had come to understand by that point that I often think aloud, and he recognised the comment as being one he need not reply to.

We had been in transit for several days by then. The *Ardent* had performed a series of jumps of planned duration while still within range of the last star systems at the tail end of the Orion arm. The idea was to give us a set of benchmark sensor readings and system diagnostics — for the effects of overlapping gravity wells of varying intensity on our specific GNG's performance — in addition to the data the ship had gathered while traversing the more densely packed star systems between the Noroconte shipyards and Wah-a-la-han Anchorage.

Other than the fact that the exit apertures of our wormholes never appeared quite where the helm officer had intended, however, everything looked completely normal. The figures were exactly what anyone familiar with such systems would expect those figures to be.

"Your people may not understand the zero thread completely," said Mol Gai, "but the way you have implemented our designs for wormhole technology is completely adequate. Lem Bataan techniques are not much different, even where we have innovated since sharing the technology with you. There should be no discrepancies in the data."

It was difficult not to take this as being patronising, given that humanity is on average at least as intelligent as the Lem Bataan, but I tried not to allow pride to get the better of me. There was no chance at all that Mol Gai had meant it that way, I was confident of that. And the simple fact is that the Lem Bataan *did* crack the problem of truly stable wormholes first. At the point when they shared their technology with us, we were nowhere near close to solving our various explosion and disappearance problems for ourselves. Since then human innovations and improvements in the field of wormhole manipulation have been very modest, simply because this borrowed technology — which we can duplicate with ease, but don't *entirely* understand — works perfectly well for our needs.

Or at least it usually does. It was actually quite comforting that the problem was also perplexing to the best minds of the Lem Bataan. That meant our own confusion was probably not due to our lack of understanding of wormholes, or our comparative inexperience with the zero thread which extrudes them. Something else was going on.

But what?

"I cannot focus my mind any more," said Mol Gai. "It is nearly the middle of this shift. We should take a break, before the duty crew members fill every corner of the mess."

"I like your thinking," I said. "We can come back to this problem refreshed."

"Precisely [Rex]."

I grabbed a new hydration pouch from the small pile I kept in that compartment and picked up my personal holo. I didn't bother to offer a pouch to Mol Gai, since I had learned — during a spectacle of an evening meal that had really taken some serious getting used to — Lem Bataan absorb all the water they need from their food. Mol Gai had made it clear that it was not necessary for me to insist on offering him pouches merely out of human politeness.

I had my personal link send a message to Zana's holo, inviting her to join us if she was able. By that point we had adopted the same shift pattern as her, and it had become the daily routine that we would all eat together if circumstances allowed it.

By the time Zana joined us in the mess, Mol Gai and I had procured food and found a table with plenty of room for the three of us. I felt embarrassed at whatever oversight had resulted in there being no furniture in the mess that could accommodate a Lem Bataan's annelid-like body form, and I had to remind myself that the navy was responsible for that error, not me.

"Wow," Zana said. "Don't you two look cheerful."

I found myself wondering how she was able to read Mol Gai's emotional state from his appearance.

"We're getting nowhere fast," I said.

"Aren't we all," Zana said. "I think *Ardent* might actually be closing on the record for distance travelled outside human space."

"Don't hold your breath," I said. "We might as well think about turning back if the research continues to progress at this rate."

Zana frowned, then laughed. "What kind of talk is that? Don't forget there are plenty of other teams working on the same problem in *Ardent*. It's not just you two."

"Think it might just be an impossible task," I said.

"Even if you are a physicist, you really shouldn't claim an absolute like that," said Zana. "And I'm an engineer, so you know if I'm dispensing that kind of advice I must really mean it."

"I don't really mean *literally* impossible," I said, "but even so, even with the resources and minds we have here... this whole adventure really is a crap shoot."

"Well besides, we won't turn back — I can guarantee you that. The captain will be fully committed by now. He'll see his part of this mission done no matter what."

"Even if we're not coming up with results?"

"Even then," said Zana. "He'll do his part to ensure that you all get every opportunity to succeed. And then later, nobody can say he didn't."

I smiled at that. It was a small but notable detail about the good Captain al-Rashid. All too often I have met people who will take any opportunity to cease their own contribution to a group effort, or to abandon a promise made publicly. Excuses are easy, resolve is not. I admired the captain's character that little bit more.

"What is wrong, Chief [Turei]?" Mol Gai said.

While I had been smiling away to myself like an idiot I had apparently missed tiny but significant gestures that even the half-blind Lem Bataan had picked up on. Zana was staring past me, the fingers on her right hand holding her cutlery in an unnatural position as though suspended in what ought to have been a fluid motion, and the fingers of her left hand pointing repeatedly past my body in a jabbing motion. I twisted around in my seat, looking over my shoulder to see what Zana was indicating.

There was a junior crewman sat alone on the table behind me, motionless, staring at a tray of food as if barely conscious of where he even was.

We all watched in silence for what felt like an age.

"You okay lil' pollywog?" Zana said.

The crewman did not respond.

"Hey," she said. "I mean *you*."

Zana threw a balled-up paper napkin at the crewman as she said that last word. It hit him square in the chest and fell onto his tray.

The crewman looked up, slowly, and his eyes locked onto Zana. After what seemed like another age he smiled, looking as though the expression took considerable effort and concentration.

"You okay?" Said Zana.

"Sure, Chief. Sure."

He went back to looking at his food, and I turned back to our own conversation.

"Is that normal feeding behaviour for humans?" Mol Gai asked.

"Sometimes people get lost in their own thoughts," I said, "and sometimes they're affected by fatigue — either could look like that."

"I don't know," said Zana. "He seemed really out of it. Mind you, pollywogs like him are usually much younger in service than the rest of the crew. He might not be used to the long haul yet."

"What does that mean? Pollywog." I asked. "You called him it straight away. I didn't come across that term when I did the naval terminology homework you almost set for me."

Zana smiled at me, I think because I was hearkening back to our very first conversation.

"Pollywog? It means someone who's not yet crossed the Deep Shadows and travelled another galactic arm. If you have done then in the eyes of the crew you're a Shadowback — much more respectable. His uniform lacks silver piping around the collar, so he's never been anywhere other than Orion arm."

"We're outside Orion now," I said. "Shouldn't he be a Shadowback?"

"Doesn't count," Zana said. "We've not crossed an acknowledged boundary into another arm of the galaxy — we're still in the Shadows and we're headed for unnamed void."

"That seems a bit harsh."

"If I understand this ritual," said Mol Gai, "then I agree with [Rex]. That is not a fair system."

"Well you two might feel differently about it if you get your way," Zana said. "He'll have to go through the initiation ceremony. He might not thank you for that."

She leaned sideways in her chair, peering around me again, and shouted.

"Hey buddy, how you feel about being— oh, he's gone."

I looked behind me and sure enough there was his empty seat, his tray still sat on the table, the untouched food congealing slowly.

"I don't think he's going to last long out here," said Zana. "The guy is pure pogy bait."

"Okay," I said. "You're just making fun of me now."

4

———

On the next duty shift I was surprised to see how quiet it was in the main engineering section. Zana was there, of course, looking far more stressed than she usually would. Given how briskly she was moving I surmised she was trying to do the jobs of several snipes at once.

"Good morning, Zana," I said. It wasn't morning of course, or indeed any meaningfully sunlight-determined period, but for everyone working our shift it was at least the start of the working day. "Everything okay?"

"No, not really," she said. "Half my bloody team is ill. Must have brought something aboard from that Deep-damned alien anchorage."

"Nothing serious I hope?"

"Not that I've heard. Most of my absentees have only reported headaches."

"They're ditching their duties just because of headaches?"

"I was cynical at first. But I've actually ended up sending a couple of people off duty too. They were acting a bit spaced out, and I don't need anyone causing an accident when I'm understaffed as it is."

"You're right, that sounds a bit more serious than just headaches."

"Yeah. The doc doesn't seem too worried, but she's still said everyone needs time to rest or she won't be held responsible for the consequences. I've gotta go by what she says, of course."

Zana pulled a rack of holographic relays out of a junction unit, caged within the plasteel frame of their sliding mount, and she placed them on a work surface. Then she stood back while she mopped sweat off her brow, careful not to let it drip all over the components.

"Have you been going full tilt all shift?"

I offered her one of the hydration packs I had brought with me. She had taken possession of her own half of the haul we acquired back at Wah-a-la-han, but I glanced around and she didn't seem to have any with her.

"Thanks. I have, yeah. Started the day a bit early in fact."

"You need to look after yourself. The ship only has one of you."

She watched me while she drank deeply from the pack, then she wiped her mouth.

"True enough. The work has to get done though, and I don't have a full team right now. You as set up for your day as I am for mine?"

The question was transparent to me and I judged that to be deliberate. As much as she probably would have liked to pass the time of day with me, Zana was inviting me to leave her to work in peace. It so happened that I had somewhere else to be anyway, but I was slightly hurt that she didn't question my presence. I had dropped by on my way to astrogation only to see her.

"Yes. I'm working with Mol Gai again. Seems to me that he's the being most likely to figure out an explanation for what's happening with your wormholes."

"And he seems to think the same about you. Well, let me know how it goes."

"I'll see you later then. Doing lunch?"

"If I get time."

I left her to her work, having learned already that her response to increasing pressure is much the same as mine. She would focus entirely on the problems before her — and rightly so, for she is a professional with a huge amount of responsibility laid across her shoulders. Though she would not necessarily *want* to neglect any social niceties, right then I would have been immaterial to her to the degree that it could have been hurtful to me. I like to think she was conscious of that.

I took my leave of main engineering and made my way through the interminable passageways of *Ardent*, taking some degree of pride in the fact that I did not once need to consult directions on a printwall before finding the section I wanted.

I was a mere four corners away from reaching the astrogation lab when I saw someone leaning over, holding himself up against a bulkhead with one hand and clasping the other to his forehead.

"Are you all right?" I said.

The figure stiffened slightly, then moved his hand up the bulkhead a little and pushed against the hard surface, twisting his shoulders around and squinting at me through puffy eyelids. Despite his somewhat swollen and reddened face I recognised him at once.

"Mister Cona," I said. "Do you need some help?"

"...Fine," he croaked.

I heard footsteps approaching, two people astride and marching in unison, and a pair of crew members rounded the nearest corner swiftly. They ignored me, went to either side of Cona, and each took an arm. He did his best to help them in helping him, placing one stumbling foot in front of the other, and they turned away quickly to take him back the way they had come.

As they moved away the man looked straight ahead. The woman turned her face to flash a brief, mechanical smile at me. Her mouth curved upwards, but her intense eyes bored into me without signalling any emotion at all. I distinctly remember worrying about the apparently unnatural degree to which she had twisted her neck in looking my way.

And then they were gone.

I hurried through the final few sections of passageway, shuttling through recent memories as I went. Try as I might I could not find any other examples of crew members aboard *Ardent* acting in such a cold and brusque manner. It was perfectly possible, I told myself, that the two crew were so concerned for Cona's wellbeing that they simply didn't have any time to spend on fraternising with a passenger.

Even at such an early stage, even before the events that were yet to come, I did not convince myself with that one.

I must have appeared unsettled in every way it is possible to do so, because I had only been in the astrogation laboratory for a few minutes before Mol Gai — a being with a self-confessed lack of expertise in human behaviour — noticed something was not right. He had been working with an astrogation holo, controlling it via yet another augment device which I presumed was authorised to interact with select navy systems, and he stopped working so that he could emulate the human convention of facing me.

"Are you well, [Rex]?" He said. "You are displaying a number of body signals I have never detected from you before."

I smiled inwardly in spite of the situation. I recalled from my earlier research that Lem Bataan are able to process sophisticated communications via scent, and I wondered just how confusingly exotic I smelled to him right now.

"It's nothing major," I said. "I just had a strange encounter with some *Ardent* crew members."

"Strange?"

"Now I think about it, it seems like it might have affected me more than it should have done."

"I can provide an objective viewpoint," said Mol Gai, "if you would care to share the details of that experience?"

"There was an ill-looking engineer in a passageway. He

was taken away by two other crew members, and it all just seemed very odd."

"An illness has swept the ship," said Mol Gai. "I believe it is thought to be mild."

"Yes, but it wasn't him who made me feel odd. It was the other two. They seemed so… I'm not sure how to describe it. They must have cared enough in some respect to come and help him, but they didn't *look* as though they truly cared about anything at all."

"Take it from me — how others look is not as useful as you think it is. There are many reasons why appearances cannot always be trusted. However you are convincing me that my own experiences today have not been misinterpretations on my part."

"What experiences?"

"I know you will perhaps struggle to understand how significant this is to me, but many of the people I passed on the way here today had the wrong scent. And in the mess this morning it was the same."

"The wrong scent?"

"Indeed. There are only a few detectable odour combinations I would expect to predominate in normal day-to-day affairs aboard one of your ships. Many amongst the crew are lacking those combinations, and they all have the same strange scent. It is stringent, and I have not detected it before. I do not believe it is pheromonal, but it *is* organic. They are emitting it from their bodies."

"I don't know what to make of that," I said. "Do you have any idea what might cause it?"

"None. I'm afraid my knowledge of human biology is not that comprehensive. The chief medical officer might have more chance of figuring it out."

Try as I might I could not concentrate on my own work after that. The experience with Mister Cona and the other two crew members kept looping through my mind, and with every pass I became more convinced that the micro-signals emanating from both of those rescuers were simply *wrong*. It was as though they were merely vehicles, being piloted by someone not used to controlling such bodies with any real skill or finesse.

I decided to go and see the chief medical officer in sickbay, but before I did so I considered that it might be worth speaking with Zana first. The matter did after all partly relate to the wellbeing of Mister Cona, and he was Zana's responsibility. When I linked through to her she answered immediately.

"Weirdly enough I was about to call you," she said, after I had explained what I wanted. "You might want to come to engineering before you go to sickbay."

Something in her tone warned me that this was an instruction rather than a suggestion, and so I left Mol Gai working in astrogation and made my way hurriedly back to main engineering. When I got there I was ushered into a small, office-like compartment, where to my surprise the ship's executive officer waited.

Zana closed the hatch behind her, sealing the three of us in the cabin.

"Okay," said the XO. "This is maybe going to sound a little strange, but have either of you noticed anything odd going on?"

Zana and I both looked at each other, then back to Commander Ouellet, and we replied as one.

"Yes!"

"Oh thank the many worlds," she said. "You haven't been ill, right? It's not marked in your files. I can trust you?"

"I've not noticed anything unusual or out of character going on with Rex," said Zana.

"Me neither," I said. "Seen anything strange going on with Zana, I mean."

Commander Ouellet thought for a moment, then looked oddly resigned, as though these answers were the best she was going to get. With hindsight, of course, I now know that was completely true.

"Before we went dark on comms we received our final databurst from the network," she said. "It updated our intel database, and included classified material about the Battle of Meccrace. I can't share the detailed conclusions of the intel analysis with you, but I can share what's in the public domain already. And my current concerns."

"Which are…?" Zana said.

"I think what happened aboard the ships of the Eighth Fleet may now be happening to us."

I knew nothing of that. I was aware of the Meccrace planetary system being a densely populated territory belonging to the Imperial Combine, but I had no idea there had been military conflict there recently. And as for what happened to the ships, and her having said it was classified material… it all sounded like something that no naval officer would normally share with the likes of me.

But the XO had started talking about it in front of me, having summoned me there via Zana, and she would have known that in no way did I have clearance to hear the things she was talking about. I presumed she had assessed the risks already, which meant that something valuable was at stake.

"What exactly happened at Meccrace?" It was certainly worth asking.

Ouellet nodded permissively to Zana.

"The entire Eighth Fleet," said Zana. "The ships. The crews. They turned on each other when the system was invaded. It *was* all over the newsfeeds."

"You know I wasn't watching," I said.

"The point is," said Ouellet, "we know the enemy has some method for influencing the decisions of individuals with terrifying precision. It turns entire crews against each other, against the Empire. I think it's started here, and in all honesty I don't know what to do. I don't know who to trust."

"Does the captain know about this?" I said.

"Captain al-Rashid was the first one I noticed acting out of sorts. He's not himself, unfortunately. We can no longer rely on him to make decisions in the best interests of the ship and crew."

I could hardly believe what I was hearing at that point. I didn't *want* to believe it. The captain had impressed me so much, with his personable, capable manner, and his refreshing strength of character, that I could hardly conceive of the *Ardent* getting along without him.

"If you know that's the case," said Zana, "shouldn't you relieve him of command?"

I may be a landlubber but even I knew the enormity of what Zana was asking.

The XO sighed. "If it were just a case of him going nuts that's exactly what I'd have to do. But I have no idea who else on the command deck can be relied upon to support that action. I don't know whether the master-at-arms is affected. I don't know whether there are enough loyal infantry aboard to help keep control of the ship.

"What I *do* know is that some key personnel are already on side with the captain, which means that others could be. Example — there's a mass shadow at the extreme limit of our aft sensors. It's been there for two days. We're clearly being tailed by another ship, but Tactical is ignoring it and Captain al-Rashid isn't interested in me pointing it out. They're probably choosing to ignore it because they're perfectly happy with it being there. And nobody is querying that.

"I hope I'm being spectacularly paranoid, I really do. But if I'm right it means the enemy has a plan in motion already, and a significant head start in implementing it. The wrong move now could propel us into a confrontation we're in no way prepared for."

Zana went quiet and merely nodded slowly at that explanation.

"And of course," Ouellet said, after a moment of hesitation, "I *could* be mistaken. I mean nobody has done anything egregiously wrong. No orders counter to the mission objective, no mysterious changing around of duties or ignoring protocols. People are just being a bit… off."

"It's not just you," Zana said. "There are enough people acting out of character to suspect something is happening aboard ship. For all we know, plenty of people throughout the Eighth had this same discussion right before the mutinies began."

Both of them went quiet, and I supposed they were thinking about what terrible things could happen next.

"I can see why you'd bring Zana in on this," I said. "She's in charge of the most critical systems in the ship. But why me? I'm not even crew."

Ouellet smiled.

"Because what I *do* have is a contingency plan. If everything does go sideways as spectacularly as it could, the Imperial Navy will probably never recover this ship, much less the black box data recorders. The likelihood is the *Ardent* will either simply go missing, or it will be turned against our own forces and destroyed.

"Comms are now fully locked out and I doubt the captain will allow that to change. We could record what's happening on holos and eject them into space, but they'd never be found in a billion years. I think our only chance to tell anyone what happened here is you, Doctor Bel-Kenita."

"Because of my condition?"

"Because of your condition. Call yourself a 'red box' data recorder. You *can* archive accurate, invariant memories, right?"

"To my implant, yes," I said. "It can also encrypt them. But I have no way of stopping that data being erased or stolen by someone if I die. It would just be a matter of time before the storage space was decrypted."

"Can you write conditional instructions into the implant?" Zana asked.

"Yes. That's a core feature."

"Then install a dead man's switch," Zana said. "If you go, so does all tactically useful data. And allow yourself to trigger that switch manually, so you can't be tortured for the data."

I grimaced at the morbid change of direction our conversation had undergone. It was not at all what I had signed up for, nor was it what I had expected when I rolled out of my bunk at the start of the day.

"We have to find a way to get him away from this ship," said Ouellet. "He needs to get back to Imperial space, preferably alive."

I favoured that option greatly.

"This cruiser carries plenty of auxiliary craft, right?" I said.

"No good," said Zana. "You'd be detected and chased down in no time."

"Yes," said the XO. "We're going to have to come up with something more subtle than that."

"There are single-occupant life pods in the aft sections," said Zana. "For crew who get cut off from the hangar bays during a ship-wide emergency."

"Small enough to avoid detection?"

"No," said Zana. "But *Ardent*'s sensors only have so much resolving power. If they were disabled across the board, just prior to launch, you wouldn't need them offline for very long before they were no longer able to locate the pod. I mean, those things are tiny."

"Erm," I said.

"Yeah?"

"Zana, I don't mean to criticise, but... are you seriously considering ejecting me from the ship, in a pod that's not capable of getting back to Imperial space?"

Zana smirked.

"Keep in mind," said Ouellet, "we're talking about a last ditch plan here. Worst case scenario."

"We better had be," I said. "Because if I get fired out into space and become irretrievable, and then everything aboard the ship gets sorted out, I'm going to die extremely annoyed."

The XO tilted her head to one side. "You may need to take that risk. Things really might get that bad."

"I—"

"Does he though?" Zana said quickly. "I think it needs to be up to him, and him alone. Rex, it's your life. You need to decide for yourself when it's time to jettison into the Deep."

"We can't leave it to *him*," sputtered the XO. "He's a civvy, Chief. He's going to need instructions. What would he know about making tactical decisions?"

Zana opened her mouth to protest, but this time I was the quick one.

"Sun Tzu. Rommel. Betombe. Scipio. Quan Tal. Napoleon. All stored up here." I tapped my temple. "Need me to go on?"

"You're not going to be strategising about capturing a valley fort with a stream, Doctor Bel-Kenita. You need real experience to deal with a situation like this."

"Give me some time to assimilate all plans of the ship, and your emergency protocols, and then we'll see how much experience I can borrow from that. I mean, those things all evolve with the collective experiences of your organisation, do they not?"

"That's a very good point," said Zana. "Like… the designs for section security hatches have been refined specifically to compartmentalise the ship. And half of our standing orders are based on what we've learned from past hostilities."

"Fine," the XO said. She shrugged in a nonplussed sort of way. "I suppose I don't have much choice at this point. Give him everything except level red."

I smiled. "You won't regret it, Commander."

"See that I don't. How long do you think it will take to assimilate all that information?"

"Depends on the volume, but my implant will help. It can

store and index data I'm exposed to without me having to understand everything I'm seeing."

"Practical upshot?"

"Imagine you exposed me to a plan of this whole deck, with sub-systems. I won't consciously recall and understand all of it, even though I store every detail. But my implant will ensure that *it* knows what is captured in that particular memory, so I can search for any specifics later."

"Okay," said Ouellet. "That's a significant advantage."

"What are we doing in the meantime?" Zana said. "In terms of not drawing attention."

"Obviously we all need to act as if nothing has changed," said the XO. "So behave as if everything is normal and maintain your usual routines."

"Even if things get stranger?" I asked.

"Especially then," she said. "You need to keep doing what you were brought aboard to do. Chief, you need to carry on with your duties as normal. I'm going to return to the command deck as though nothing is amiss."

"And then what?" Zana said.

"What do you mean?"

"Are we just going to wait around for things to deteriorate, or are we going to investigate? Surely if something actually *is* happening it will just get worse and worse. If we want to prevent a catastrophe, we need more information."

"I don't know what you think we're going to do," said Ouellet, "but if you have any suggestions, please do make them. Personally I think we should be expecting the worst, and if it comes to it all of our efforts should go into sabotaging the enemy's plans."

"Even if that's suicide?" Said Zana.

"Even then. Realistically, what else can we do? If we somehow gain control of the whole ship, we'll have to hold it for almost a Solar month before anyone comes looking. Can we survive that long, holed up somewhere? Can we maintain control, without free access to the areas where systems could be diverted away from us? I'd say not."

I looked at Zana and saw her brow knit as she worked furiously on that problem. Her whole expression dropped after a few moments.

"I guess not. But still, we need more information. Otherwise we're just waiting for the enemy — if they are taking over — to start making decisions for us. If that's what we're doing we might as well all be under their control anyway."

"Conceded," said Ouellet. "What would you suggest?"

"Well first things first, if there's anything in that intel of yours about how the enemy does what it does, we need to know about it."

"The indication from other suspected incidents is that there's a biological agent that's the root cause. People who are affected usually have visible symptoms to begin with, similar to a mild flu. There may also be confusion, and repetitive actions without real purpose."

"And the rash of symptoms sweeping through the crew would support that. So the doc needs to weigh in on what she thinks is happening."

"Ah, very direct. The engineer's approach. What happens if she's one of them?"

"Then what she tells us will stand out, because she'll lie and it will probably make no sense."

Ouellet's mouth drew into a thin line, and she nodded slowly.

"The master-at-arms," she said. "We need to know if he's affected too. Because if he is, we're going to need a plan for getting our infantry friends to take orders from someone else. That might be problematic."

"One problem at a time," I said, "is the only way to deal with that situation."

"Indeed," said the XO. "I guess I will be the person best positioned to speak with him. It will look suspicious if either of you try, whereas I can camouflage it as routine ship's business."

"I'll speak with the doc," I said. "I can create my own cover easily enough. If I'm pressed I'll just say my augmentation is giving me problems."

"Good," said Ouellet. "Zana, I think you're best positioned to assess Beta and Gamma shifts. I've not been able to keep a close eye on them, and we need to know how many personnel are still fit and capable. If anything does happen, and *we* end up being the ones mutinying, the ship still needs to be staffed."

"I'll switch up my own shifts," said Zana. "Work across the teams. There are enough absences right now that that will look completely understandable."

"Not really sure why you aren't doing that anyway," said the XO, "but I suppose this isn't the time for a performance review."

"I'm holding this ship together pretty much on my own."

"I was making a joke," said Ouellet. "Perhaps not the right moment."

"You can say that again," I said.

"Well we all have our assignments. Doctor—"

"Just Rex."

"As you wish. Rex, please do be extra careful. I'm acutely aware that you're a civilian, and a guest, and I don't want you exposing yourself to serious dangers."

"Flippant dangers only. Very well then."

Ouellet stared at me for a long moment, wearing an expression of pure bafflement, then turned her attention to Zana.

"That goes for you too, Chief," she said. "Be on your guard at all times. If I'm right we're in serious trouble, and nobody is coming to help."

"Understood," said Zana. "You can count on me."

Ouellet nodded and left the compartment briskly, and with that the first meeting of our conspiracy was ended.

"Are you okay with this?"

"How do you mean?" I said.

Zana tilted her head to one side as she regarded me with her quizzical engineer's expression. It seemed as though she was trying to work out a puzzle, to work *me* out.

"What?" I said. "Go on, just ask me."

"I'm really not sure if you're going to be up to this. Sneaking about and possibly being in peril, I mean."

"I'll be fine, Zana. Rest assured I can lie with the best of them, should the need arise."

"Because you always remember exactly what you've told people," she said. "Okay, that makes me feel a little better. But what if you get yourself into physical danger?"

"Then my only plan will be to run away, terribly quickly."

"Perfect. I'm now much less worried."

A short time later I left Zana figuring out how she was going to achieve her own objectives, and I set off back to astrogation. I had no intention of going to sickbay without backup, given that there was now nobody aboard ship I could trust other than Zana, Mol Gai, and to a certain extent Commander Ouellet. It had also occurred to me — in the time since the XO told me about events at Meccrace — that what Mol Gai may have been detecting in the ship's recirculated air was literally the scent of treason.

If these people were being affected biologically, and that was what caused them to act against the interests of the Imperial Combine, then maybe the odour Mol Gai had described was also a product of the same process. If so, those individuals might as well have painted themselves hot pink and run around screaming. They were detectable.

So yeah, there was no way I was going to go prying in sickbay without a Lem Bataan by my side.

I arrived back at astrogation to find Mol Gai engrossed so deeply in his work that he barely registered my arrival.

"Getting somewhere?"

"[Rex], welcome back," he said. "I think I have something."

"Can it wait for a while?" I asked. "There's something I need to do, and I'm going to need your help with it."

"Wait?" Mol Gai stopped working and directed his full attention at me. "But [Rex], this is the whole reason we are here. To find a solution to the wormhole problem. I may have narrowed down the search considerably."

I opened my mouth, intending to tell him that now we had a whole new problem, but stopped myself just short of speaking. It occurred that Ouellet had said nothing of bringing anyone else into the fold. She had not forbidden it either, but then discretion was not only implied in the plans we had discussed, it was explicitly demanded by them. And as much as I liked Mol Gai, he was a representative of a foreign power. Who knew what political impact it might have if I passed on information about insurrection within the very ranks of the Imperial Navy?

"What have you found out?" I said. Now, of course, I wish I had been more brave.

"I decided to take a parsimonious approach," he said. "I have treated this the same way [Zana] would treat a problem in one of the ship's components."

"Intriguing. Go on?"

"What do we know? We know that the gravity needle generator is working fine. It is the same as Lem Bataan generators, and we have no problems. We know the colli-mator rings are working fine. They are the same as Lem Bataan collimators, and we have no problems. We know your navigational software is working fine. It is substantially the same as the Lem Bataan nav system, and we have no problems."

"You've narrowed it down to one specific thing, haven't you?"

"I have, [Rex]."

"You sly and wonderful being. I think you've been downplaying your achievement a little here, my friend. I can't wait to hear this. Please do enlighten me."

Mol Gai seemed to draw up his mass, becoming more upright, and I wondered if humans and Lem Bataan share the same physiological impulses when we are immensely proud.

"It is not exactly a problem with hardware," he said. "I believe the problem is in your mapping. That is the only part of the system in which humans and Lem Bataan do things differently."

"And something has gone wrong with ours."

"Hence your wormholes are affected, but ours are not."

"And nobody has thought to check that before, because—"

"—because the accuracy of maps does not usually change so much over such short time scales."

We had performed no simulations, checked no data, consulted no charts — and if Mol Gai had done so before I got back, he didn't tell me — yet I felt sure that he had cracked the problem. His answer explained so much. Everything, in fact, that needed to be explained, without requiring any logical consequences which were absent in reality.

"You know, I told Zana I thought you'd be the one to crack this case, and there you go. Genius."

"You are too kind, [Rex]," he said. "It was simply a matter of eliminating elements. The simple approach is often the most effective."

"Tomorrow then," I said. "We concentrate entirely on demonstrating your hypothesis. I've not heard of anyone else coming up with anything so compelling, so I'm sure the captain will provide all the staff and sensor time we…"

Now, it's difficult to imagine how I could have got so carried away that I forgot the predicament which was unfolding at a horrifically slow pace in the compartments and passageways of the ship. I suppose the simple explanation is that at the time the physicist in me was actually getting excited.

"Is there something wrong, [Rex]?"

"No, I'm... just thinking about the logistics of what we're going to have to get done."

"I have started to compile a list of requirements already," he said. "I have dictated it to the systems holo in here, but I will transfer it to your personal device."

"Thanks," I said. "We can go over it at dinner, if you don't mind mixing some work into our downtime."

"No, I do not mind," said Mol Gai. "Not for something like this. It could be the breakthrough we have all been looking for."

"Let's hope we get to do something with it," I muttered.

If Mol Gai wondered what I meant by that, he never said anything about it.

5

Zana skipped our evening meal, and it took a few surreptitious rounds of messaging her from my holo — secreted in my lap as I sat opposite Mol Gai in the crew mess — before I was convinced that the person writing back to me was not an enemy agent. As she had promised to Commander Ouellet, she was moving her sleeping pattern forward so that she could overlap more easily across the night and morning shifts in engineering. She would have eaten her 'evening' meal about four hours before we ate ours.

Having suggested a working dinner, I then had to feign deep concentration while plodding through a number of dry data comparisons. Mol Gai was as animated as I have ever seen him, and as he began to propose semi-speculative experiments designed to show that Imperial mapping was not what it used to be, I found myself wondering how it was that even a Lem Bataan could not tell fake enthusiasm when he saw it.

I felt bad that I did not feel immediately invested in his ideas and his work. He had, after all, made what was probably the most significant leap forwards since we had all come aboard. But at the back of my mind was a shadow, and in my gut was the constant worry of wondering who was watching, listening, and possibly scheming.

By that point the idea that something was wrong in the ship was beginning to weigh on my mind, fringe my perceptions, and colour everything I did and thought. After all, it was no longer merely a matter of me being unable to explain oddities and peculiarities in the behaviours of what was essentially a closed group of people, people who might simply have their own idiosyncrasies and all be used to seeing them in each other. No, that was not it at all. At least two members of the crew — both of senior rank and each with a capably analytical mind — had seen the same behaviours for what they were: difficult to explain, and ultimately sinister.

I ate hardly anything at that meal, and when Mol Gai had finished ingesting the wet, glistening mush which had been prepared for him specially, we left the aptly named mess and headed towards the forward sections of the ship.

"I still need to go to medical," I said. "There are some concerns I have about this illness everyone seems to be catching."

"I will come with you," said Mol Gai. "If you do not object, that is. I am worried that the illness might not be accounted for in the vaccinations I have received."

"No, I don't object at all," I said. "In fact I was going to see if you would come anyway. There's something I need to ask of you."

"What is it, [Rex]?"

"I'd like you to not mention those unusual smells to the corpsmen in sickbay. And after we leave, let me know if you have smelled anything strange emanating from *them*. Or any of their staff, for that matter."

There was a long silence while Mol Gai took this in.

"Something is wrong, isn't it [Rex]."

"I'm afraid it might be. But I don't want to worry you unnecessarily."

Another long silence.

"I assume you are withholding the details because this is an issue relating to Imperial Combine security."

"Very possibly. I've been asked to restrict the spread of information."

"I see," said Mol Gai. "I must admit to feeling a little disappointed. We are colleagues in science, and our people are allies."

"I'm sorry, Mol Gai. I don't mean to offend or upset you."

His flanks rippled, just noticeably.

"I cannot pretend, however, that I do not understand," he said. "Since I have similar standing orders of my own."

"You do?"

"Any Lem Bataan visiting Imperial Combine worlds, ships, or facilities, must first undergo contact training," said Mol Gai. "There is a standardised course which was devised by the *Soor-Ais*. It is delivered by the Academy of Sciences."

"I hadn't realised we were still considered that untrustworthy."

"Do not misunderstand, [Rex]," he said. "Humanity is certainly a trusted ally of the Lem Bataan Confederation. But there are many amongst my people — I think you call them 'hardliners' — who believe we should never have shared any technology with you. They are influential. And now the policy that has been adopted by the state is to prevent any additional sharing of technology. That policy is enforced to the level of individual contact."

"You're telling me that you aren't allowed to suggest or explain anything we don't already know about?"

"That is correct. And I will be debriefed when I return to Lem Bataan space."

"So what happens if this navigation issue requires, say, one tiny piece of hardware that we simply don't have?"

"I would not be able to assist. I can only work with the technology you already know about, and I can only use problem solving techniques that rely on established logics. I must also stay within the limits of your collective scientific knowledge."

"How do you know when you're straying outside those bounds?"

"That is the stupid part, [Rex] — a lot of the time I have no idea."

I laughed openly at that, catching myself by surprise as much as Mol Gai.

"Well I certainly don't resent your discretion in any way," I said. "You're as much subject to the rules of your people as I am to the rules of mine."

We had been walking while we talked, and we were now almost at the section which contained the sickbay proper and all of its ancillary compartments.

"I can't get into the reasons now," I said, "but are you willing to do as I asked?"

"I am, [Rex]. I do not believe you would act badly, and I do not believe you would mislead me into doing so."

"I'm glad to hear it."

"But I would like to think you will explain at some point soon," he said. "I do not enjoy undertaking labours for others without knowing the reasons why."

"That's perfectly fair," I said. "Remember — not a word of the unusual odours you've been detecting."

"I will remember. It is simple."

We entered sickbay, and I was surprised at just how far back into the deck the compartment reached. It was one of the largest single spaces I had seen since coming aboard the *Ardent*, and that included both the mess and the cargo bays.

"Can I help you?"

One of the medical staff approached us across what I assumed to be the reception area. His plain, white smock, with a single caduceus symbol on the left breast, was strikingly different from the duty tunics worn by virtually every other crew member I had seen so far.

"I was hoping to speak with the chief medical officer," I said.

"The CMO is currently engaged," said the nurse. "May I ask what it's regarding?"

For some reason I had imagined I would be able to waltz straight into sickbay and speak directly with the corpsman in charge. Apparently I had been a touch naive about that.

"I'm an Augment," I said. "I have some concerns about my implant."

"I am perfectly qualified to run diagnostics for augmentations," he said. "If you'd like to come through to the cybernetics ward, I'd be happy to—"

"That's very kind," I said, "but I'm afraid I really do need the corpsman to take a look for herself."

"May I ask why?"

The nurse looked put out, and I felt a little guilty about implying that his skills or knowledge were not adequate. Perhaps my ruse had not been the best I could have picked. My mind rattled through a number of potential ways to develop the lie in a way that helped him to save face, as well as advancing my aims.

"This is a little embarrassing," I said, "but you've actually caught me out. I'm not ill at all. I'm carrying information for your CMO."

The nurse's face told me everything I needed to know — initial mild surprise, followed by what was clearly a combination of fascination and satisfaction.

"That sneaky... I *knew* she was working on a new paper. She's been denying it since we left Noroconte."

"She is, yes. Big secret. Please don't tell her I told you."

"What is it? Go on, you can tell me. She's using the crew as a cohort, isn't she?"

"I really can't say," I said. It was difficult to not smile, so I didn't try. "Of course I don't necessarily need to deny anything, either."

"She *is*. Ooh, I'd better not be one of her test subjects too.

What is it she's looking at, effects connected to prolonged missions outside dense stellar neighbourhoods?"

"Something like that, yeah," I said.

"Bit pedestrian."

"I suppose that's her prerogative," I said. "Anyway, think you could…?"

"Of course," he said. "Come this way."

The nurse ushered me across the sickbay, not once questioning why I had a Lem Bataan in tow, and waved me in the direction of a hatch at the end of the leftmost bulkhead. He pressed the panel next to the hatch, and waited.

"Yes," came the reply, eventually. "What is it?"

"Visitor for you Doc," said the nurse. "Special case."

There was a long pause before the tired, querulous voice sounded again.

"Don't know what you're talking about."

The nurse looked at me with an expression which told of great forbearance, and slapped the door control anyway. The hatch slid open and he stepped into the space. The lights in the compartment were set relatively low, and I squinted into the gloom as he explained.

"This gentleman has an implant issue," he said. "He's asked for you specifically. Said you would definitely want to look at it."

The nurse was placing emphasis on certain words, in a way that would only have made sense to the corpsman if she had been expecting an Augment to turn up carrying secret information to her. I tried not to laugh.

"What *are* you talking about?"

"Well I'm sure I don't know," said the nurse. He winked at me, and then turned to go. "I'll leave him with you."

The hatch slid shut behind him, leaving Mol Gai and me in the half-lit gloom of what appeared to be a madman's office. It was as disorganised as Captain al-Rashid's, but with a very different feel indeed.

"Who *are* you?" Said the corpsman.

"Forgive the intrusion," I said. "I was hoping to talk to you in private, and your nurse wouldn't let me in without a good reason. I told him I was carrying data for you."

"I see," she said.

She stood up, leaning against a desk, and turned up the lights a little. I saw that she was a middle-aged woman, prematurely grey but clearly accustomed to keeping an athletic figure.

"But why are you *really* here?"

She scrutinised me, and I stared back at her. Her eyes were deeply set, bloodshot and with slightly yellow bags under them. She leaned on the desk as if for support. Her free hand trembled a little. This was someone who had not slept properly for some time, and I was confident I knew why that might be. I decided to take a leap of faith.

"To talk about the problem with the crew," I said.

"It's just a virus."

"Not the superficial problem," I said. "The real problem."

Now her eyes really bored into me.

"What do you know about that?"

"I know it begins with the headaches," I said. "And I know it ends with people who aren't themselves."

"I don't think we've seen yet how it ends."

"I also know there are people on the bridge who are affected, and I'm guessing that's why you're locked away in this cabin. But you're not alone in this."

She looked at the deck, and there was a long pause before I heard her tremulous voice again.

"You're part right. People are changing because of it. I'm sure you know what happened to the ships mustered at Meccrace, and there's a chance that will happen here too."

"Part right?" I said.

"I'm not in here to keep myself safe," she said. "I'm in here to keep myself from harming anyone."

"You're infected."

"I... am."

"How long for?"

"Day two, I think," she said. "I feel very strange."

"And are you still yourself?"

"As far as I can tell. But also not convinced. Imagine standing by a river, and just barely hearing someone call out to you over the sound of the rushing water. That's how my head feels right now."

"How disconcerting," I said. In all honesty I did not know what else to say to that.

She moved around the desk, supporting herself hand over hand with the edge of it, and I moved out of the way. I heard Mol Gai shifting backwards behind me.

The doc seemed to notice Mol Gai for the first time when he moved aside for us both, and she pointed at him.

"Immune, that one, I shouldn't wonder."

"Are you sure?" I said.

"It's a virus," she said. "We know it affects humans. Probably won't recognise his cells. Fundamental differences. There aren't many human pathogens that are compatible with Lem Bataan biology — that's why immunising them is such a trivial task."

"I have not felt any different since this all began, [Rex]," said Mol Gai. "I think the doctor is right."

"Seems like we have an ally here," I said to him. "It's probably fine to mention the odours."

"It is so strong in here, [Rex]. It has been very difficult to stay silent."

"What's that?" Said the corpsman. "Odours?"

"My Lem Bataan friend here is smelling a strange scent emanating from some of the crew. We think people who are infected might have a unique smell."

"Don't see why not. Perfectly possible, medically speaking. Looks like you have yourself an early warning system."

"You smell very strongly," said Mol Gai.

"None taken. Like I said, I think this is day two of the infection for me. It'll be affecting my biochemistry for sure."

"Do you have any idea how long it takes to run its course?" I said.

"Not sure," she said. "But from what's happening amongst the crew I don't imagine it can be much more than three days. Not long for me now."

"Any idea when and where this started?"

"That I *can* tell you. It was in the water. I've had the storage tanks sterilised, but it was too little too late. Everywhere now. Sterilisation should've been done the moment we left Wah-a-la-han. Shouldn't have relied on their people to have done it for us. Have to make an issue of that when we get back. If I get back. New protocol needed there, I think."

She moved across cautiously to a couch positioned against the bulkhead, and sat down before rotating her body and lying down gingerly.

"In the water," I said. "From when we had our tanks topped up."

"Yes. Everything that was still in the tanks from Noroconte would have been swept twice before we reached Wah-a-la-han. This infection must have come aboard at the anchorage."

"Do you think that could have been deliberate?"

"If it *is* the same thing happening here that happened at Meccrace, then I'm certain of it."

"I've been using hydration packs instead of the potable water supply," I said. "Do you think I'll be okay?"

"Probably not," said the doc. "You might have avoided drinking from the main supply, or used it boiled, but that same water is also used for the things you're not thinking of. Rehydrating food matter, supplying faucets, providing showers... you've had contact with it whether you realise it or not."

I grimaced. So much for not using the recycled water.

"However," she said, "if you've not been quaffing great bucketfuls of it like the rest of us have, it might take a lot longer for this thing to affect you."

She sat up again, looked at me thoughtfully, and pressed her fingers into her brow as if trying to massage out a headache.

"You might even be the last of us to remain yourself."

Besides everything else that was said before Mol Gai and I left the corpsman in her self-imposed isolation, and parted ways ourselves, that comment above all others weighed on my mind the most. I felt so tense and worn out by the time I got back to my quarters, that I barely had the energy to update Zana before falling into a deep slumber.

It was first thing in the 'morning' of our next duty shift when Mol Gai noticed something very obviously amiss. I did not see it myself while I was still in my cabin, nor whilst I was making my way through eerily quiet passageways to the *Ardent*'s crew mess, but once we were seated it was not long before my dining companion asked me to turn around and look.

"Am I mistaken," his translation device relayed, "or does nothing outside appear to move? I know my vision is not the best — you may see things differently."

I turned and looked, and sure enough the view outside was of an apparently static star field. Faint and banded, sure, thanks to our position relative to the spiral arms of the galaxy, but definitely about as fixed as such a panorama can possibly appear. When a ship is travelling under conventional drive the stellar scenery does not streak by blisteringly fast, as some planet-dwelling folk might imagine it does, but even at low cruising speeds the field of view would usually be changing sufficiently that one could notice with only a glance.

The crew mess only had a few people in it, and barely any of them were talking. Nobody paid any attention at all to the view outside, nor expressed any curiosity as to why we were not moving. One crewman — sat all the way on the other side of the mess from us — stared directly at me and hummed a mournful harmony to himself.

I shuddered. It was becoming increasingly difficult to pretend that everything around us was normal.

We abandoned our plans for breakfast and headed instead to main engineering, where we found Zana frowning intently at a holo. I noticed that the ranks of her engineering staff seemed even more depleted than they had on the previous day, yet today she seemed as though she was less flustered and more single-minded. She was *really* staring at that holo.

"What's happening," I said. "Do you know why we've stopped?"

Zana didn't look up from her device. "There's another ship."

"Out here?"

I could barely believe anything else would be out this far from any star system of value. I mean sure, *we* had our reasons, and so accordingly might someone else have reasons of their own. But the chances that two such wandering craft would happen across each other? Vanishingly small. And the XO had said she thought we were being followed by another vessel, one that had been hanging back at the periphery of our sensor field. It seemed obvious to me already that this was not a chance meeting.

"Whose is it?"

"It's one of ours," she said. "A corvette. Bridge isn't responding to my queries, but I've got it up now on exterior monitoring."

"This mission was supposed to be only us," said Mol Gai. "I do not understand."

"Neither do I, and that's concerning." Zana swiped at her holo and plucked several panes of information out of the image of the other ship. "It's the *Hector*. I'm sure that name rings a faint bell."

"Like the prince from ancient myth?" I said.

"If you say so," said Zana. She continued to swipe and tap. "Here it is, I knew I'd heard that name come up recently. This was posted to all commands as an urgent bulletin. The

ICS *Hector* was stolen from Fort Kosling, about the same time all that business started with the Viskr."

"Stolen?" Said Mol Gai. "If you have had no bulletin to say it was found, surely that means— oh, that is unfortunate."

"Yeah," said Zana. "It means whoever's aboard probably doesn't have our best interests in mind."

"Do you think that is why your command deck has not responded to you?" Mol Gai said. "Because they are managing this as a crisis?"

"I really doubt that," said Zana. "*Ardent* and *Hector* are both aligning themselves for hard connection by umbilical. I think this whole cruiser really is being stolen out from under us."

"Commander Ouellet," I said. "We need to make contact with her, and urgently. She could be in danger."

"Think perhaps we could *all* be in danger," Zana muttered.

"Yeah, I agree," I said. "But think about where she is. If people are stealing this ship, and they have the guts to act so brazenly, surely they know perfectly well who's on their side on the command deck? She's completely exposed."

"Damn it," Zana groaned. "You're right. We need to get her away from the bridge."

"Might you call her down here?" Said Mol Gai.

"Could do, but that would be like sending up a flare to lead them right to us as well."

"What about some other location?" I said. "We could direct her to a false emergency situation somewhere, meet her, then get out of there quick."

Zana tilted her head to one side. "I think that's probably the best we're going to be able to do."

"Can such an emergency be simulated?" Said Mol Gai.

"I'm a career engineer in the Imperial Navy," said Zana. "I spend quite a lot of time imagining things that can go wrong."

"But one that would demand her presence?" I said. "In a convincing yet controllable fashion?"

"More or less," she said. She smiled wryly. "I may have had some slight sabotage protest fantasies in the past."

"We need to get this done quickly," I said. "If you create and control the emergency, I'll go and fetch her."

"Are you sure?" Said Zana. "I can't imagine this will be at all safe. Don't forget you're not actually a part of this crew, Rex. You don't have to stick out your scrawny civilian neck for anyone."

She was smiling faintly as she said that, but I could tell she was being sincere. As much as I would have liked to remain safe within the relatively fortified capsule of the main engineering section, behind pressure hatches and emergency containment bulkheads, I could not help but feel by this point that I had some degree of responsibility towards the people I knew were still themselves. And as the doc had suggested in sickbay, I might yet find myself the last person aboard able to do anything about the situation. Perhaps it was time I started to take a more active role in what was unfolding around us.

"Did the commander get back to you about the— what did she call him? The master-at-arms?"

"No, not yet."

"And if I understand what she was getting at, he's the guy who keeps order aboard the ship?"

"Yeah. He's navy, but he's technically in charge of the infantry contingent we're carrying. They're supposed to be like military police while they're under his command."

"And right at this moment we don't know if he can be trusted."

"Not yet, but we can find out for ourselves."

"Not quickly enough to help Ouellet," I said. "We need to act now, and if we can't guarantee his affiliation then perhaps it would be best if I went."

"I really don't think—"

"If the master-at-arms is affected, or his soldiers, they

might not be that interested in me. Taking over the ship means taking over the crew, not passengers. I might get away with slipping past people, but if you go you're going to be far more vulnerable."

I could see from her face that as unhappy as Zana was with the thought of me sauntering off cheerfully into dangers unknowable, she saw the logic of how I was approaching the problem.

"You had better take Mol Gai," she said. "If he's happy to accompany you, that is?"

"I too would prefer [Rex] to not go alone," said Mol Gai. "I will help."

"It might be safer overall if it's just me by myself," I said. "The fewer of us who are exposed the better."

"And then what if something happens to you?" Zana said. "Who's going to tell me?"

"[Zana Turei] is right, [Rex]. We can no longer wander the passageways of this ship unaccompanied. We know now it truly is not safe."

Zana crossed her arms. "You're *not* going on your own."

"Fine," I said. "Have it your way. Mol Gai, I'd be delighted to have you along."

Zana smiled. If Mol Gai was smiling I had no idea how it was being represented.

Mol Gai and I made our way out into the passageways of the ship once more, this time aiming for a section which Zana had determined was likely to be relatively understaffed in the usual daily routine of interstellar transit. She had shown me where it was on her holo, rotating the three-dimensional plan of the ship so that I could derive its position relative to engineering in all axes, and I had memorised a number of alternate routes right away.

My link chirruped, and I checked my holo before answering. It was Zana. I clicked my link once and accepted her call.

"I've found the perfect spot," she said. "Manifold junction I can blow out. That'll light up holos across the command deck. If Ouellet has any sense she'll tell al-Rashid not to worry, and volunteer herself to come check what's happening."

"Great stuff," I said. "And what about us?"

"How do you mean?"

"I can't imagine the XO will be the only person who takes an interest in investigating a mysteriously well-contained explosion."

"You'd better hide until she turns up."

"My thoughts exactly," I said. "Any ideas?"

"You're the one who memorised the deck plan, smarty pants. You want to be near junction three-delta-fourteen."

"Fine," I said. I loaded the images from her holo into my working memory and skipped through the unhelpful parts. "Got something. General supplies storage, hardly any distance away from that junction. We'll be there in a few minutes."

"I'll give you five," she said. "Then it's game time. Good luck."

The link went silent, and I saw that she had ended the connection.

We approached two crew members, one tapping at a printwall, the other standing still and staring at an area of the bulkhead which displayed no information at all. Both Mol Gai and I fell silent the moment we saw them, and I could almost feel him bristling with discomfort as we passed. The one who had been tapping the display controls of the print-wall turned her head to watch us until we disappeared around the next corner.

"They both had the scent," said Mol Gai.

"I knew you were going to say that," I said quietly. "Not far now."

We reached the supplies compartment at last, and entered swiftly before anyone else who might see happened into the same passageway. The compartment was compact, with a central bank of shelving and storage racks on all the bulkheads. Webbing and clamps braced components and various kit containers against the racking.

We had been concealed within the small compartment for mere moments when I heard a loud 'bang' somewhere further up the passageway, followed immediately by a *whummmph* sound, and a clattering noise like some piece of metal casing skittering along a passageway. A siren began to honk intermittently, and red light pulsed in the recessed status strips of every bulkhead, close to the overhead, even within our little storage cabin.

I opened the hatch slightly and got as close to the gap as I could without revealing myself. I peered through the crack and watched what happened in the passageway outside.

Thunderous footsteps came swiftly and alarmingly from one side, and I withdrew sharply as a blur of motion flew past the gap. I overcame my instincts and pressed my face back into the gap, twisting to see down the passageway. It was the crewman I had seen a short time before, the one who had been staring at blank bulkhead. Now he stood in the middle of the passageway, stock still, staring as a jet of pressurised gas invisibly but noisily breached the scorched valve which would normally contain and control it. The crewman cocked his head one way, then the other, then simply left.

While I had watched him my heart had been practically in my mouth and my breathing had almost halted. There had been something almost feral about the way he had approached, and the jerky, predatory quality of his body movements, but at the same time everything about his behaviour seemed sort of detached. It was as though he had been sent out from a central mass as a scout, sent out to *seek* on behalf of that greater body. My skin had crawled as I thought that.

I waited for a few more minutes before I called Zana.

"One person came," I said. "Looked almost inhuman, the way he was. He left pretty much right away. No sign of the commander, I'm afraid."

"Damn it," said Zana. "Okay, I'm going to have to take a bit of a risk. I'll alert the bridge to the problem and *ask* for her to come down and inspect it."

"How long before this leak becomes toxic?"

"It won't."

"Couldn't it still displace all the breathable air?"

"That'll take a while," she said. "But if it makes you feel any better I'll restrict the flow to that section."

"Thanks," I said.

"Okay I've got a response back from the bridge," she said. "Not from her — it's from COMOP. Simply says that the command staff are currently engaged with a situation of their own and they're unable to attend to minor mechanical issues. The problem falls within engineering's remit and I'm to handle it."

"So much for that plan," I said.

"I think she's stuck with them, yeah," said Zana. "Come back. We'll have to think of something else."

"Link to her directly?" I said.

"I'm not sure we're that desperate," said Zana. "Not yet. Seems like if she *is* okay for the moment, that would put her at risk. And if she isn't okay, then it puts us at risk for no reason. Just get back here and we'll come up with a new plan."

We left the storage compartment, quietly and cautiously, and stole back up the passage the way we had come originally. At the next junction I was confident enough in my understanding of the deck plan to take the opposite path from the way we had come. Anyone seeing us come back the same way we had approached, after all, might rightly conclude that we had had some involvement in an unexplained incident with some escaping gas.

We had been travelling in silence for several minutes — sometimes passing crew members and other passengers, most of whom looked oddly disinterested as we went by — before we reached an intersection with a major trunk passageway.

Mol Gai stopped dead, and looked for all the many worlds as though he was peering into the depths of the trunk passageway. Knowing his rudimentary eyes were simply not that good, I assumed he was trying to focus the maximum power of his sensory augmentations.

"What is it?" I said.

"I do not know, [Rex]. Not exactly. But something here is… wrong."

"Wrong?"

"Yes," he said. "I do not want to use this corridor."

"What do you see?"

"Nothing," said Mol Gai. "But I smell it. And I *know* that something is here. I doubt my translation device can explain how."

I peered into the passageway for myself.

The corridor stretched away from us, unerringly straight, its plain, metal bulkheads and occasional printwalls as inoffensive and unremarkable as those of any other passageway in any other ship. The light fittings were placed at helpfully predictable intervals, hatches were evident here and there and seemed well behaved, and where plasteel panels had been pigmented to act as decor they were coloured with muted, calming hues. There was nothing at all wrong that I could see.

And yet, somehow, all the tiny hairs on the back of my neck were standing on end.

The silence in that passageway was oppressively deafening. The longer and harder I stared into it the more dimmed the edges of my vision became. The distant convergence of my perspective became a brown-black, tarry blur, the straight edges of the carpeted deck buckled outwards, and I began to see floaters in my peripheral vision. The more focus-distorted my vision became, the more my intuition told me that the passageway was staring back at us with cold eyes of its own.

My scalp prickled.

"I don't know why," I said, "but I think you're right. I feel like… like there's something there."

"I do not want to go that way, [Rex]," said Mol Gai.

"Oh, I'm with you on that," I said. "Believe me. I guess we'll just have to backtrack."

We turned and left the intersection, heading back the same way we had come, and I reviewed the deck plans again for an alternate route. After that strange moment, whether anyone was about or not, all the way back to engineering I had the eeriest sensation that we were being watched.

6

It was not long after I had selected a new route back to Zana that she called me again on my link, letting me know that *Hector* had decoupled and departed. We reasoned between us that the corvette had likely been transferring personnel or items aboard *Ardent,* since we were not carrying anything of obvious value.

"You might want to use an alternative entrance to main engineering," said Zana. "Main entrance is off limits for now, but I'm sure you'll find your way back safely."

"What's happening?"

"Got some company," she said. "Think we know exactly where the master-at-arms stands now."

"Is he there?" I asked.

"Not in person, no," Zana said. "But he's sent a bunch of guys here to take up positions in engineering. They're saying they're meant to be additional security, but I don't like it one bit."

"Are they with you now?"

"No, I'm keeping them occupied. Left them outside and closed the hatches. Told them I need to clear their orders with the bridge before I allow weapons anywhere near the main reactors."

"Good thinking," I said. "Can't imagine that will stall them for long though."

"No, I'd had the same thought. Get back here quickly."

"What do you think *I'm* going to do about them?"

"Nothing. That's not why I need you back here. Look, I don't want to discuss it over a link. Just in case anyone is listening in."

I didn't think that was very likely — the level of encryption built into links is absurdly high, and mine is not a navy-issued device. But I said what I needed to say to stop her worrying, then I shuttled through my memories of plans and schematics to find anything like a secure back door into engineering.

I quickened my pace, and I heard the *hiss-click* of Mol Gai's respiratory augmentation accelerate in frequency as he raced to keep up with me. He was surprisingly quick, but I felt bad making him rush for no adequately explained reason. As uncomfortable as that must have been for him, however, he didn't complain.

It took what felt like an additional forever to circumnavigate the entire engineering section, but we got around to the aft-most bulkheads eventually. It was a strange environment. Whereas on other decks the section would have contained numerous passageways and compartments, here the space was primarily occupied by huge conduits and relays passing from the main reactors to the conventional drives. Deck plating and parts of the inter-deck structure were absent in many areas, with bunches of thick conduits and giant manifolds winding around each other and passing through chamfered gaps in cross-deck bulkheads. Despite the mechanically confusing landscape it did not take long for me to find an auxiliary maintenance access hatch, such was the accuracy of the deck plan in my head. I linked to Zana, gave her the hatch number, and asked her to unlock it remotely.

For once it was Mol Gai whose mode of locomotion was an advantage. By the time we emerged into an aft engineering chamber, through another access hatch, I was beginning to feel claustrophobic. Muscles I rarely find myself using in the usual tasks of everyday life were screaming at me that I should leave them alone.

Zana did not meet us as we crawled from the narrow maintenance shaft. As soon as we were back on our feet — literally for me, figuratively of course for Mol Gai — I hurried through to the overview stations. A handful of engineering staff were still in the main compartments, each and every one of them with stunned expressions etched permanently across their faces, and I wondered what they thought exactly of everything that was going on in the ship.

I found Zana right where I expected her to be, which was glued to her principal control holos. Her eyes kept flicking from a display showing plans and data, to one which showed a surveillance view of the main entrance to the engineering sections. On that security holo I saw men and women dressed in the same fatigues and — worryingly — with the same combat armour and rifles as those soldiers who had extracted me from the surface of Kementhast Prime. These were clearly a contingent of the infantry carried aboard the *Ardent*; from what Zana had said they were not part of the crew, not even Navy personnel, but must have been seconded from the Conventional Air and Ground Assault force. The soldiers were waiting outside the primary hatches leading into engineering, and they wanted in.

Zana glanced up as we approached her. "Boy, am I glad to see you," she said.

"What did we miss?"

"Nothing much since I asked you to get back here," said Zana. "Which is weird. They're being unusually patient — by now I would have expected lots of calls on my link demanding my compliance."

"They're all armed, I see. I thought guns won't fire aboard ship?"

"The suppression system can be shut down fully from the

command deck, or selectively by a master-at-arms. Wouldn't be very helpful to have all our weapons offline while we were being boarded."

"Good point," I said. "What's the plan then?"

"I don't think I can keep them locked outside forever." Zana sighed heavily. "The logic as I see it runs like this. If they're all affected by this thing then they probably know that *we* aren't. By now they may have learned I've made no effort at all to contact the bridge and verify the orders. Even if not, they will know soon that I'm stalling. If I continue to stall, they get in anyway eventually and the people in here will be 'dealt with' decisively, whatever that will turn out to mean. If I let them in now, after what is simply a delay, it may be we're left alone for a bit longer, which isn't much but it does at least give some more opportunity for monitoring and sabotage."

I couldn't fault her logic. There were some unknowns in there, more of them than she had truly acknowledged, but the flow of reasoning seemed sound.

"So what are we doing?" I said. "Just giving up?"

"No," said Zana. "Firstly I *am* going to contact the bridge. I'll go through the charade of authenticating these orders."

"Justify the delay, and create doubt about the idea that we know what's really happening."

"Exactly. And the second part of my plan is for you."

"Me?"

"You." Zana waved a hand towards the rear of engineering, then on seeing my confusion she pointed out the hatch to a specific compartment. I noted it was extremely close to the shaft Mol Gai and I had used to return to engineering. "I'm giving you access to level red, never mind what Ouellet thinks about it. All the data we hold on our restricted systems, secure authorisations, and classified technologies."

"Wow. And then what?"

"Then you go out the way you came in, and you make yourself scarce. Like the commander said — you're the contingency plan. Stick to the sections of the ship people don't generally go into without good reason. Stay out of sight, out of mind. Wait until you think the moment has come to use the information I'm giving you."

I had begun to move towards the other compartment already, while she was talking, but now I just stopped and stared at her. I was not sure at the time how to respond to this scale of responsibility. She must have seen the look on my face for exactly what it was.

"I'm sorry to put this on you, Rex," said Zana, "but I don't know what else to do. From what Ouellet and the doc have said this crew will soon be fighting itself for control of the ship. No single person has a comprehensive knowledge of all systems, which means nobody can win without a war of attrition. Might means right. You're going to have to be a circuit-breaker. A weapon of last resort."

"I'm really not much of a fighter," I said. "I don't know what good you think I'm going to do out there."

"Don't get me wrong, when I say 'win' I'm not expecting you to fight to take back the ship single-handed. I think Ouellet's expectations are more realistic."

"You mean lose the ship, but on her terms?"

"Yeah. If you think it's beyond hope that the ship might be retaken, you make damned sure it can't be used by the enemy, and then you evacuate yourself from the occupied territory."

All of a sudden there was a large, cold stone where my stomach would usually have been. My scalp prickled — not as much as when I had seen the odd seeker peering at a gas leak as if he had expected to find floundering prey, and then had an entire passageway stare into my soul, but still enough to make me shudder in response.

"What about Mol Gai?"

"What do you mean?" Zana said.

"He's probably immune to this thing. Will he fit into one of our escape pods?"

Mol Gai twisted his head towards Zana.

"I am also curious to know the answer to that," he said.

"Honestly?" Zana said. "I doubt it."

"What would you suggest?" Mol Gai said. "I do not wish to stay here if the ship is taken by these people."

"I really don't know," Zana said. She looked even more dejected now than when she had told me I would likely become the final option for any resistance. "Let me wrap my head around that problem while we still have some time. I'm sure I'll come up with something."

"Don't doubt you for a moment," I said. In all honesty I was not that confident she would come up with an idea that wasn't excluded already by the parameters she had cited when talking about my own possible futures earlier on, but I wanted to give Mol Gai some indirect encouragement.

"Thank you, [Zana Turei]."

"You're welcome. For now I'd suggest you also find some-where to lie low."

"I'd really like him to stick with me," I said. "Seems as though he can identify the people who are affected."

"It'll be harder to go undetected, if you're moving around as a pair," said Zana. "And you each have different needs. If this situation turns into a prolonged stand-off then you'll be at greater risk trying to keep yourselves provisioned."

"Nothing we can't think our way around," I said. "The advantages outweigh the risks."

"Well I can't very well stop you," said Zana. "But remember what's at stake. You still need to be prepared to push the button, so to speak."

"I won't forget," I said.

"[Rex]," said Mol Gai. "I want to preserve my work before it is too late. If we do get to return home, we will need to take that data with us. I will go to astrogation."

"Let me get the level red package assimilated, and then I'll come with you."

"I wouldn't wait," said Zana. "Time is of the essence. This whole thing could go sideways with no warning at all."

"Safety in numbers though," I said. "Like before — we both went together to the leak. What if something happens to you? Who would know?"

"I agree with [Zana Turei]," said Mol Gai. "[Rex], you must absorb the information about the critical systems before we lose control of engineering. I must retrieve my data from astrogation before we lose the ability to move about the ship freely. We must not squander time if we do not know how much time we still have. We must work in parallel."

"Couldn't have put it better myself," said Zana.

"If you insist," I sighed. "But please do be careful, and get back here as quickly as you can. Same as before — use the maintenance shaft."

"I will," said Mol Gai. "Before I leave, there is one more thing we need to discuss, [Rex]…"

The Lem Bataan's translation device somehow did a good job of indicating that his speech was trailing off with unspoken import, and he turned his face towards Zana briefly before returning to face me.

"What's that?" Zana said. "You can tell me directly, you know."

Mol Gai seemed to shrink down slightly, in a full body gesture which looked like the polar opposite of the drawing up of mass I had seen when he had been proud of an accomplishment.

"You are certainly infected, [Zana Turei]," said Mol Gai. "It is likely that you too will turn against us."

Zana closed her eyes, leaning against the plinth of the console below her holo. Her lips became thin, and I was certain this was to stop them from trembling.

"I know," she said. She opened her eyes. "Told myself I just had a tension headache… from all the extra work, and moving my sleeping pattern. But it's not that. I'm going. Slowly but surely, I'm going. I am."

I found myself completely at a loss as to what I should say. I am not the most sociable of people by any stretch of the imagination, and while I had come to like and respect Zana quickly that did not bestow me magically with skills I did not have beforehand. I have shied away from difficult situations before, especially those surrounding illness, death, or other bad news. My fondness for Zana must have been one of the most genuine attractions I have ever felt, because it was in that moment I realised that my lack of preparedness for a situation like this was precisely because of my deliberate avoidance of similar situations in the past. All of a sudden that mattered to me. Experience was lacking, as they say. I had no choice but to try and find the right path by feeling my way.

"We'll find a way to reverse this," I said. "There has to be a cure."

Zana looked at me reproachfully, and I started to regret my choice of words almost immediately.

"Please don't make promises you can't keep," she said. "It sounds like a platitude. I don't need platitudes right now, I need assurances."

"I'm not very good at this sort of thing," I said. "Sorry."

"I can tell. But I don't mean I need you to assure me about my future, not like that at any rate. What I need is to be sure that whatever happens to me, *you're* not going to do anything foolish. Nothing that would put your own survival at risk."

I thought I knew exactly what she meant, but still I hoped she had thought of something I hadn't.

"Do you mean—"

"Don't act out some idiotic heroics like coming back and trying to get through to me, as though all you have to do is remind me that we're friends and then somehow I'll over-come this thing and be normal again."

"Right."

"It's not a holo-film we're living in here. Stunts like that will end us all."

"But there has to be something—"

"You don't come back for me, Rex. Just don't."

There was a long silence. After a moment Mol Gai crawled away without saying a word. Zana tapped on her holo to open the maintenance hatch for him, and he disappeared into the shaft beyond it. I presumed the discussion was over, and prepared myself mentally to start absorbing huge files of information at speed. I now had lost time to make up for.

"The doc said it was in the water," I said, "but we've both been drinking from those packs. So we're going to be the last to turn."

"You need to make sure you're in one of those pods before it happens to you," said Zana. "Hard limit on that. Don't take a chance with it — we can't risk you becoming one of them too."

"I know," I said.

"If I think I'm really going, I'll make sure I can't interfere with your plans."

"What do you—?"

She touched me gently, slid her hand down my arm and then squeezed my fingers.

"Oh. You mean…"

"When you're done, let me know," said Zana. "We'll say our goodbyes."

She turned and walked away briskly, heading towards a hatch to a compartment which neighboured the control area. My memory record is very specific about the fact that there was a tear sliding down her cheek as she turned away from me.

I had been staring at a holo in the side-office as intently as I could for a good half-hour before I heard a strained conversation coming from the main compartment. The voices were raised, with both sides clearly trying to assert themselves, but I could not detect any of the sort of verbal aggression that would usually signal immediate danger.

The soldiers were inside engineering, then. I wondered if that was because Zana had run out of ways to stall them, or if it was because she had come around to their way of thinking at last. As if answering that very question she sent text to my link, and without looking away from my main display I flicked the message from the edge of my personal device and onto the holo in front of me.

> Will hold them here. Go out the way you
> came in. Inner hatch is not locked. Reply
> when you're done and I'll distract them.

I increased the paging rate of the work station, pushing the limits of how fast I can take in data. The quicker I was done there, and back out into the rest of the ship, the less chance there was of being caught. Oh there were more crew outside engineering than there were soldiers inside, sure, but it's all about encounter rate. Engineering at that point was a concentrated spot of potentially hostile eyes; the rest of the ship at that same moment was mostly empty passageways.

The data on the screen changed and changed and changed.

The funny thing about people's reactions to hearing of my augmentation is that they think the advanced specifications of the technology are responsible for all the benefits. They sort of are, but at the same time it's also the case that the technology is exposing the true extent of human specifications. If my brain could not remember things for itself the implant would do nothing of any use. For the most part the main advantage the implant gives me — as a side effect of its intended purpose — is guaranteed accuracy of storage at heightened input rates, which it does with frightening efficiency. A secondary benefit is that it also archives and indexes anything I deem to be 'particularly useful'.

Since all of the information I was viewing was categoris-able as 'particularly useful', that meant my augmentation was having to do a lot of additional processing. It was telling me through the optical feedback loop that processor temperature had increased by a noticeable percentage — not the first time that has ever happened, but it was still worrying — and I had to keep a metaphorical eye on that meter as well as the task I was trying to stay focused on.

I was very glad that the XO had asked Zana to give me access to data about the ship's hardware and protocols, as well as crew procedures, ahead of time. The level red package was fairly dense, and if I had had to absorb everything in that one session I think my brain might actually have melted.

At long last a final screen's worth of data flashed up, and when I advanced the display there was nothing more to show. I sighed, and tension I had not even been aware of fled my muscles.

> Done here. Ready to go.

There was a long pause, longer than I would have liked. I could still hear muffled voices occasionally, drifting through the open spaces of the main engineering compartment and somehow penetrating the hatch to the small office I was using.

> Wait twenty seconds then leave. You stay
> safe out there.

> Thank you Zana. Stay safe. I hope we meet
> again.

> Me too, Rex.

I followed her instructions, counting in my head far more accurately than she probably would have expected. At the count of twenty I opened the hatch of the cabin as quietly as was possible, and very slowly stuck my head out through the gap. At the far end of the main compartment, still near the overview stations, I saw Zana talking with a small group of soldiers. She was holding their full attention somehow, and I took the opportunity while it was there.

I sneaked silently from the side office and back to the

maintenance hatch, slipping into the shaft beyond and taking one last look at Zana Turei before the hatch closed after me.

She looked my way and our eyes met. I waved in what I felt was a mournful yet hopeful way — perhaps experiencing the emotions for myself more clearly than I expressed them with my hand — and she continued to speak and gesticulate as though nothing had happened. There was not a flicker across her facial expression, such was her dedication to the task of distracting the soldiers.

Or at least, I hoped that was the reason for the lack of emotional response. I told myself that were she turning to their side already, she would likely have pointed at me and yelled. The metal sheets and grille plates of the maintenance shaft felt particularly cold as I crawled away from the last friendly human with whom I was likely to converse. I wished then, without any precedent except maybe scenes from holo-films I have watched in days long gone, that I had held her and kissed her when she touched my arm.

Emerging into the strange, technological hinterland behind the aft-most part of main engineering, I crawled out of the maintenance hatch in an ungainly fashion and got to my feet as quickly as I could. I stole cautiously to the first corner, peered into the passageway beyond, and then began to move. The sooner I reconvened with Mol Gai the better.

I used my previous experience of navigating towards astrogation through the grid of the ship's corridors, noting which routes had been the most heavily travelled where members of the crew were concerned. It was impossible to also plot a path which did not pass any of the laboratories or research compartments in which passengers such as myself would be labouring, but I was able to factor those in and find a route which reduced the number I had to come close to.

Eventually, after ducking into a few compartments to avoid encounters, and false starts where I had believed it safe to continue only to have some lone person appear silently around a nearby corner, I made it to the astrogation lab. I had not called ahead over my link for fear of unknowable surveillance — despite considering my link and Mol Gai's comms device safer than those of the crew, there was a reasonable chance that the broadcasts would still be detectable in some way. I also did not want to risk giving away Mol Gai's position at an inopportune moment with a blast of unexpected noise.

The hatch opened, and the first things I noticed were a peculiar, pungent smell, and the fact that all the lights were off. I entered, tripping the sensors which brought up the light levels, and found myself retching immediately.

What confronted me was a charnel house.

Pieces of what I could only assume were internal organs were strewn across the deck, and piled at the foot of the far bulkhead. Some kind of creamy, pink-grey fluid was spattered everywhere, pooling around what looked like a great, leathery sleeping bag left open to dry in the sun.

This unwrapped carcass had been Mol Gai.

Unable to stay standing, I sank to my knees and tried to prop myself up with my hands. One palm slipped in the juices on the floor, and I recoiled in abject horror, flicking a string of sticky fluid away from me frantically. I tried not to look at the body while I waited for my head to stop spinning, but my eyes kept going back to it, feeding images into my brain which will now never be forgotten.

It was then that I noticed exactly *how* my gentle, intelligent friend had been slain. It was not from a series of many stab or slash wounds that he had been split open, and there was no ragged laceration that would speak of a frantic effort to saw him apart after death. No — one continuous, straight incision along his belly showed he had been sliced open cleanly, perhaps even in a single motion.

As grim as this analysis was, I tried to cling on to its clinical sterility and enquiring nature. I knew I had to get back to my feet and escape from that place, and I could not have done that while my legs were beyond conscious control. I had to hold on tightly to that investigatory mindset while I copied Mol Gai's data from the astrogation holo. I had to put aside my revulsion and the desire to sink into grief, and move.

Seems like we have an ally here, I heard myself saying to Mol Gai. It felt as though that had been days and days ago. *It's probably fine to mention the odours.*

We had told the doc ourselves about his potential tactical advantage, knowing full well that she was turning. I had instructed him to do that. They knew he was a threat to their plans, because of *me*. Tears stung my eyes as I got to my feet at last, and I slapped at the panel to open the hatch.

"Shame, really a horrible shame. He was quite brilliant."

The XO was standing right in front of me, slap bang in the middle of the passageway outside the astrogation lab.

"Commander Ouellet," I said. "Are you…?"

"Free of my duties on the bridge, for the moment," she said. "I wasn't able to get away before. I assume that stunt with the gas was for my benefit?"

Her underwhelming reaction to finding a butchered passenger aboard ship had been an immediate red flag. With that question though it seemed obvious she was probing to find out if I was part of a counter-movement.

"What stunt?"

She smiled thinly. "Come now. Trying to get me to come down here. We had to stop to pick up another guest. A VIP, you know. It's always a demanding process — security and all that."

I began to edge out of the astrogation lab's doorway as subtly as I could, trying to get my body into a position from which I could launch it down the passageway outside.

"Security?" I said. "We're hundreds of light years from the nearest hostile territory, surely?"

"As we've discussed, Doctor Bel-Kenita, not all threats are external."

She tilted her head in a birdlike fashion, and I knew right away that she too was measuring how much of me was still inside the hatchway of the lab, and how quickly I would be able to jink around the jam of the opening and start actually running. Her apparent lack of concern told me exactly how much danger I was still in.

"You said a VIP," I said, hoping to shift her attention. "Out here?"

"He had to come here," she said. "He brought the singers, and the chorus, and a mouth for our mind. Now we can all be what we need to be."

"I… what?"

"He's eager to meet you, Rex. He's come a long way."

I didn't need to hear any more, and I chose that moment to make my bid for freedom. I burst past her, leapt into a run, and hurtled down the passageway as fast as my unaccustomed legs would carry me.

"I'm not chasing around after you," she yelled. "It's demeaning."

Good, I thought, as I leaned hard into the first corner. But then the last thing I heard her shouting after me sent a chill down my spine.

"We have polybots for that sort of thing."

I pumped my legs harder. I have seen military polybots in action on the news feeds, and her suggestion that one was about to come after me told me exactly how Mol Gai had been killed. An apparent single killing blow, opening him from throat to tail? Only a polybot would consider that to be a reasonable solution to the problem of him being alive, and also be capable of carrying out such a precise physical act while compensating for the thrashing of its victim's body.

Yes, it's fair to say I ran faster and farther then than I ever have before.

A crew member lunged at me from a hatch which opened even as I passed by it, and I brought up my arm instinctively to protect my face. My elbow caught him in the jaw and sent his head sideways, banging it off the edge of the hatchway, and down he went. I found my stride again and continued, my lungs now starting to burn.

Another crew member, caught by surprise as I rounded a corner, and one decent, two-handed shove put her on the deck. I was gone before she could get back to her feet.

Left. Right. Ladder. Left, left, right. Hatch. I consulted the deck plans constantly as I ran, picking out a nonsense route which brought me ever closer to the relative safety of the aft engineering spaces but gave no chance of predictability.

Gradually the sounds of other shipboard life faded, until only the quiet, steady hum of life support was audible over the thunderous beating of my own heart, and I found a storage cabin in which I could sit and gather my wits while my burning lungs soothed themselves and my heart rate came down from heights hitherto unexplored.

I am not ashamed to say that I also had a little cry.

7

———

After what felt like a long, long time, when my hands had stopped trembling and I could no longer hear my own blood rushing through my head, I left my temporary hiding place and headed out yet again into the passageways of the ship. This time I felt far more vulnerable than at any point beforehand. With hindsight I imagine this was because I no longer had a fixed refuge, a place to think of as sanctuary against the dangers of open corridors and uncertain corners. At the time though I recall that I believed both the number and the severity of the dangers had escalated.

I no longer believe that. Now that I can look back on everything that happened, I can draw reasonable conclusions about the steps which must have taken place for things to end the way they did. The vicious murder of Mol Gai had been a specific expression of the violence the enemy was always capable of, not a change in how violent the enemy was willing to become. Certainly the danger to us all increased when the *Hector* arrived, bringing with it the catalyst necessary for the *Ardent* to be fully under His control, but many of the events which threatened me directly could have happened right from the start of it all. It only would have taken the circumstances to be ever so slightly different.

But they weren't, and when I found myself running scared and alone through the passageways of a now hostile star cruiser, the large differences really did not matter to me any more than fine distinctions would.

I kept Zana's instructions in mind. She had told me to disappear amongst the more predominantly mechanical areas toward the aft end of the ship, somewhere between the engineering section and the actual interior housings of the conventional drives. It made sense — unless maintenance or emergency repairs were necessary, nobody ought to be hanging around in those areas. The risk of random encounters was much lower than it would be on the parts of the decks dedicated to habitation, work, or recreation.

She had also said that I should pick my moment.

I wondered how I would know when that moment had come. Was it upon me already? Everyone I had thought I could rely upon was gone, and nowhere seemed secure. Was it time already to try to rob the intruders of their prize?

It very much appeared so.

I found myself another quiet corner, hidden behind a large, steel manifold which emerged root-like from a bulkhead, split into three parts, then took a ninety degree bend and disappeared collectively down through the deck plating. I waited for a few moments, listening for any small sounds which might give away a stalking pursuer, then began to review filed memories.

Somewhere around here, I thought, *there will be an access station capable of letting me do some real damage.*

There were a few options available to me, as it turned out, for denying the intruders possession of the entire ship. The most definitive method would be detonating all the primary reactors like bombs, in an explosion that would also ignite the xtryllium coils built into the ship's gravity needle generator. That would have been quite spectacular, ensuring beyond all doubt that everyone aboard the ship was dispersed into the great dark as little more than a flash of energy. In all likelihood, the gravitational reaction of the ignited xtryllium would also have resulted in the immediate locality no longer being classified as navigable space.

Two major issues with this plan made me dampen my enthusiasm. Firstly, there were so many automated failsafes designed expressly to prevent just such an occurrence that it seemed at best like it would mean a great deal of unnecessary work, and at worst it would prove downright impossible to arrange. Secondly, I was not convinced that my little life pod would escape the blast. Of course I could use some sort of timer, but that meant taking the risk that my efforts would be undone by the mutineers or intruders, or some automated safety system, after I had ejected myself with no way to return to the cruiser.

Another option would have been launching all the ship's drones and having them riddle the hull with holes — they could in theory all be slaved to a single control station. But then the crew of the ship, despite their unusual mental state, would be able to use the C-MADS turrets to shoot down those drones, probably with a much higher rate of fire. I might potentially be able to keep the drones within the minimum firing arc of the defence turrets, but I wasn't confident enough that I could actually do that to risk everything on the attempt.

Like the primary reactors, air composition was a system that was tamper-resistant by design. With the detection of any large shift in the proportion of gasses present in the breathable mix, mechanical features inherent to the design of the system would cut in to push the ratios back again. There was no way to override that safeguard, and when I tried to locate the firmware functions that had responsibility for detecting such changes — a system I thought I could probably modify fairly easily — I found that the software engineer had made it all so complex and labyrinthine that I would need days with a diagnostics holo just to figure out what might work. It was very clear that the code was written that way deliberately, and I did not have days.

And then… yes, that was it. That was exactly what I needed.

I found something intriguing, while scanning down through the maintenance and overhaul protocols, and even though triggering this process would cause wholesale slaughter I am ashamed to say that in that moment a smile formed on my lips.

If I could just convince *Ardent* that he was in dry dock, and that it was time for a complete interior overhaul, I would be able to open all exterior and interior hatches at once. The atmosphere of the ship would rush out into the night in a tormented extrusion of gales, taking some crew with it and leaving the others with nothing to breathe. Anyone managing to keep themselves sealed safely in a compartment would be trapped there by the lack of atmosphere everywhere else.

As horrifying as the idea was it was also the only chance I had to keep *Ardent* from falling into the hands of this enemy force. I would be fine, whether I triggered the final event while waiting in my life pod, or found a small, hidden hole from which to preside over the final death of the ship. I preferred the former idea, since it meant I would likely not accidentally witness anyone being killed by my plan. Although by this point I was sure that everyone else in the ship was now the enemy, I had no desire to watch their last facial expressions as they were pushed out into vacuum by their own ship's atmosphere.

I also considered the grisly possibility that my pod might bump and bang its way through flotsam bodies upon ejecting from the ship. Unlikely, given the sheer size of the ship's perimeter, but still not a pleasant thought.

I raced through schematics and sets of protocols, viewing the steps taken by the crew and the mechanisms triggered in a variety of scenarios. *Ardent* would believe he was in dry dock only if certain conditions were met. The magnetic grips on the fore personnel airlocks had to be in reception mode, and needed to be linked and sealed with the airlocks of a maintenance stanchion or docking pier. Similarly, the exterior clamp hard-points had to be folded out and connected to the dry dock superstructure. Lastly, the ship required confirmation of a handshake with the dry dock facility's control deck. Only then would the all-hatch release function be permissible.

One by one I rattled through ancillary processes, contingency plans, disaster recovery protocols, and maintenance routines, working outwards from everyday events to the unusual and extreme scenarios, until I found two of the three solutions I needed.

The airlocks could be dealt with using a basic workaround — I would simply tell the ship that all of the airlocks were closed for repair. Airlocks which have been powered down for repair do not need to be connected to a dock, and cannot be activated for safety reasons, so they would in theory be ignored by the automatic docking routine.

The hard-points for the exterior clamps were also easy to deal with in principle, because they could simply be folded out. The ship would not check if a dry dock stanchion had extended its own clamps and bitten down on the hard-points of the *Ardent*, because it was the responsibility of any such dry dock to make those checks for itself before handshaking with the ship. The problem as I saw it was that extending the hard-points would alert everyone on the bridge — the operations and helm stations would tell their respective operators that the ship was preparing to dock.

Maintenance mode. Of course. A tiny entry displayed in a small file at the very edge of the docking protocols map. Bless the hearts of all engineers — in their world even a chunk of metal on a hinge gets to have a maintenance mode, and because they don't want fellow snipes being yelled at every time they tinker or tweak, maintenance mode naturally reports absolutely nothing to the command deck.

The last hurdle was the most difficult. How to fool *Ardent* into thinking that a dry dock facility was saying 'hello and welcome'? I was thinking about this problem when the first announcement came, prompting my heart to leap into my mouth. I call it an announcement because that is, in meaning and in effect, precisely what it was.

"I am now concentrating entirely on finding you."

The voice was broadcast across what I assumed was the ship's integrated public address system, and I heard it coming from two different directions at once. That, combined with the creepiness of the unaddressed non sequitur, made my skin flush cold all over.

"It would be very helpful if you would make your whereabouts known."

I wondered what pursuit had been taking place, which unlucky member of the still unaffected crew had drawn the specific attention of the person speaking. For a moment I tried to identify the voice by comparing it to recent memories, but I had no luck in matching it to anyone I had heard talking during my time aboard the ship.

Whomever it was being addressed I could potentially use their plight to my advantage. While they drew the attention of the others I could perhaps start putting practical elements of my own plan into action. If the right number of coincidences occurred, at the right times, there might even be two of us ejecting from the ship in life pods.

That, of course, assumed that everything would go to plan. I had enough experience of experimental design to expect that at least one thing would not turn out the way I might like, so I reviewed alternative options quickly, and applied some creativity in the ways I imagined that ship's procedures and human life could be interrupted as efficiently as possible.

"There really isn't any need to make this difficult, Rex."

My heart stopped, and somewhere in the space above my mind a supernova exploded darkly. The nebula it left behind was shaded by dusty veils of confusion and dread.

The voice had named me.

I moved. There was nothing else I could do. This person — whoever he was — was looking for *me*, and I had to act. If there was ever a time to put my plan into action it was now. Staying put and hiding in that tiny, dark corner felt like the safest option, but if someone was actively searching for me then in reality it decidedly was not safe at all. No, I had to kill the ship and leave by the back door, before I was found.

I scanned through memories once more, looking for an auxiliary control station, and found there was one not far from where I had been hiding. It was buried within the aft sections of this deck, in amongst all the bundles of conduits and giant junction boxes which helped keep this great machine moving.

Finding it was easy, and with access to level red getting past the holo's security layer was a simple matter indeed. It was not long before I had all the airlocks in the fore sections marked as being out of order, and the exterior clamp hard-points folded out as though awaiting inspection. The last step — telling the *Ardent* that it was docked at a friendly space station — was a little more troublesome.

A drone. I could use an element from one of the earlier plans I had considered, and have a drone transmit a facsimile of a dry dock's handshake transmission towards one of the cruiser's comms antennae. I might not even have to launch the drone, but if I did it would surely be easier to evade the point defences on *Ardent*'s hull with one drone than it would be with a cloud of the things.

I tried to access the relevant systems from the control station, but the holo informed me with surprising curtness that it was for engineering purposes only, and could not be used for tactical functions. I searched my mental map of the ship again and found the nearest launch bay. It was not too far away, and only one deck below me.

It was when I was in motion once more that the voice began to follow me again.

"Where are you now? Every time I think I have your position, you're somewhere else."

I carried on, not caring if the owner of that voice was trying to mislead me or being sincere. There was no way to know, so I was certainly not going to start second-guessing my decisions.

The farther I moved back in to the main body of the ship, the more shouts and screams I heard. Occasionally, the sound of small arms fire rang around the passageways.

"Do I really need to have everyone else remain still, just to find the one person who keeps moving about?"

That question did almost make me stumble, as I faltered in my stride but my feet fought to keep going. If the voice was capable of doing that, any hatch I opened between compartments would be like a shrieking alarm on the bridge. I had no choice though but to go on.

A lateral maintenance shaft gave me the chance to sneak across the deck, avoiding the likelihood of random encounters, and I took that chance gladly. I was reasonably sure that opening these minor hatches would not trigger status indicators anywhere, and I could find nothing in my memories of ship's systems to suggest that they were alarmed.

It was while I was in the maintenance shaft that lights began to go out. Now don't get me wrong, the shafts are not exactly brightly lit and welcoming to begin with — they have the faintest and most economical form of low-energy light possible, presumably with the expectation that service engineers will bring their own lighting, but that their portables might from time to time fail on them. The point is that even when light is very, very faint, it is far preferable to none whatsoever. And none whatsoever is exactly what was coming.

I did not notice at first, because I could not see behind me as I climbed horizontally across the deck. But when the lights around me were extinguished, followed by those ahead of me, and then the next set and the next, I cottoned on. I looked past my feet and saw nothing but an inky blackness, a blackness that now was all around me. I lost sense of direction and scale, and could only think to keep moving forwards. The shape of the shaft would have to be my guide.

As I moved forwards again I heard a faint clinking sound. I stopped, and so did the sound. I moved again, and there it was. *Clink-clink-clink-clink.* As before, it stopped when I stopped.

I brought my arm up and turned on my holo, dialling up the brightness. Green-blue light filled the immediate vicinity of the shaft, colouring the metal walls and dropping off quickly in the empty dark ahead of me.

Clink-clink-clink-clink.

It was difficult to localise the sound, and so I had no idea where it was coming from, but I had definitely not moved that time and could not have made the noise myself. I shunted my hips across to one side and did my best to shine the meagre light from my holo back down the maintenance shaft, the way I had come.

Red and blue dots shone unblinkingly back at me.

The dots plunged forwards, and the metal face of a polybot was pulled by them into the pool of graveyard light cast by my holo. It released an inhuman sound as it approached me, like a shriek of victory, and its metal limbs now clattered and banged as it lunged towards its prey like some angry, asymmetrical, metal centipede.

CLANK-CLANK-CLANK-CLANK.

I did not wait for a single millisecond longer, and crawled away as quickly as I could, using every corner and junction I could find. The polybot was fast, but only on the straights. On corners its motion became less fluid, and to negotiate them it had to reorient those segments of its modular body which carried irregular tools. The first couple of times it had to learn how to navigate the spaces, which slowed it down considerably. I lost ground, I gained ground, I stayed just far enough ahead to avoid its grasping fore-claws.

I came to a four-way junction, panting and sweating, and

the light from my holo disappeared into the depths of each of the three exits I could choose. I was about to turn right when tiny, red and blue lights blinked into existence from right to left — somewhere down that shaft another polybot was stalking silently. I looked left, and saw more or less the same thing. My only option was to forge on ahead.

The next maintenance hatch could only have been a few meters away from that junction, but when I found it I felt as though I had been crawling for months. I spilled out of the shaft, tumbling onto the carpeted deck of a passageway, and locked the hatch from the outside.

Feet greeted me.

"Hello, Rex. I've been looking for you."

I looked up slowly, not wanting to prompt any hostility from whoever this new face was.

The man was standing no more than a couple of meters away, in what I can only describe as a casual stance. His wiry, chestnut-coloured hair, his dark, smooth skin, and the distinctive melody of his accent suggested he might have hailed originally from the colony at Imiron, although his clothing, expensive and tastefully appointed, was of a style more usually found on High Cerin. He was average in every way I could describe him — build, height, looks — and appeared to be in his mid-forties, by my estimate. He smiled as though we had not seen each other for a long, long time, which I suppose in all accuracy we had not.

"Who are you?" I said.

"I don't really have a name of my own. I've been given far too many, by many different creatures. Some of your people call me 'Voice', if that helps."

"Voice? What kind of a name is that?"

"The sort of name they give to one who speaks, I suppose. But it's just one among many, as I said, and more flattering than others I've been given. Feel free to add a new one — I'm not picky."

"What do you want?"

"What huge questions you ask."

He smiled more widely, and the expression made me feel uneasy. Everything about the movement of even the tiniest facial muscles seemed authentic enough, and his eyes shared the smile, but all together it just felt *false* in a way I could not explain.

"I mean with me, with this ship."

"Well you see Rex, I have a problem. My problem is that you people have a problem. All of you. You just can't seem to pull in the same direction, no matter how dire the necessity. Right now the necessity is really very dire. I won't worry you with the details, not right now, but broadly speaking you can take it from me you're on course to all go down together. And if you all go down, I go down with you. I don't want that Rex."

"What has any of that got to do with me?"

"I think you will be a real help to me, Rex. You and your unique properties. I think you can really change things up. I think you will help me to transform trillions of doomed lives."

"I have no idea what you're talking about."

He smiled an unnervingly wide smile. "Have you ever been a vital part of something bigger than yourself?"

With this sudden change in direction and tone, I became curious about what it was this strange man really wanted. It was not merely a case of him being a threat — clearly he had a more intricate motive, and whatever he wanted from me there was now some indication that ensnaring my physical form was not going to be enough. He wanted me to understand something, I was just not getting it, and he was now taking a different approach. I wondered what weaknesses he would expose if I played along.

"Depends on your definitions," I said. "If you're talking about a choir, or a professional sports team, I'd have to say no. If you're talking about the more abstract engine of academic research, then yes. Why do you ask?"

"Your terms work for me. How does it make you feel, when you contribute to the body of knowledge that will create your civilisation's future?"

"It's okay I suppose. I leave thinking about the future to others, but I do know what you mean. I have a friend and colleague, Doctor Ber— well, she's of that mind anyway. She *is* concerned with how future generations will remember our work."

"But you are not?"

This time it was my turn to smile. "I just need to find the answers. Solve the mysteries. The problems need solutions."

He nodded several times, and raised a hand which he then used to punctuate his words, gesturing towards me in a way that felt as though he was trying hard not to be too aggressive as he emphasised his points.

"It's time you thought about the future, Rex, and the problems it contains. There is a great silence out there, and it is growing towards us. I intend that not one of us should disappear into it. We will fill it with living sound instead. Will you help me, Rex?"

"I don't know what you're asking of me."

"Join something larger. Sing with me, with us all. The harmony is exquisite. I want to hear you within it."

"I'm now even less clear about what you mean," I said. "If this is your sales pitch then I'm afraid it's losing me."

"You would become a part of *me*, Rex. You would join with all of us, with what we are and what we contain. I am now billions of us, and this communion we share is the greatest forge of computational creation to ever exist in our galaxy. Be a part of it Rex. Make the new world with us."

Something in his earnest appeal caused pieces to slot together in my brain, and I realised all of a sudden what the evidence pointed to. This person in front of me was not just another man. He was not convincing anyone to join his cause as individuals. This body was merely a representative of the thing that all of them together had become. It was as much an individual amongst a whole as one of my fingers might be considered an ambassador for the rest of me, which is to say not at all. No, this thing *was* the whole, communicating with me through a mere appendage.

"You're a gestalt organism," I said.

"You could say that. Though I do think that rather clinical term does rob some of the beauty from us, if I'm honest."

This is the enemy, I thought. *It's what we're at war with. This thing kills fleets.*

"Beauty? I don't know about that. I hear you've caused carnage on the Orion arm."

The man stopped just short of smirking, then tilted his head as if weighing me up afresh.

"Carnage is a harsh term," he said. "Oh there have been some robust encounters, certainly, but I think people like us are above worrying about all of that."

"People like us?"

"You in particular are regarded as one of the finest minds in all the many worlds."

"I—"

Anybody else would likely have missed that, but I of course am unable to forget. Within a second of him saying it I had connected the phrase to earlier memory, and the realisation that he had used the exact words of Captain Mansour al-Rashid, with the same intonation, made me lose entirely what I had been about to say.

"Three doctorates from two of the top academic institutions in Imperial space. Very impressive, Rex."

A gestalt organism. It had incorporated the captain, and everyone else. It *knew* what they knew. The game had changed suddenly, and I confess my knees felt weak. I raced through memories of conversations and lines of sight between me and others aboard ship, checking for any advantage this creature would have if it had indeed absorbed all of the people with whom I had interacted.

"All that work. Tell me, were you close?"

My blood ran cold when I matched that to memory. Those were the exact words of Doctor Berris.

"You… you've been to Kenita-Deng?"

"I'm there now," he said. "I started to take that facility before you had even left Kementhast Prime. It's mostly mine already, although I'm more of a people person than a machines person. I leave crafting and operating things to people like yourself."

I stared, not knowing what to say.

"I like Euelli. She's not so simplistic as others. She has a lot of faith in you, you know. She wasn't joking about giving you a whole new facility."

"What *exactly* have you done to her?" I sputtered.

"Nothing horrible," he said. "She has begun to sing the song. She will make a world. Euelli Berris is adamant that you will be the one who helps me the most."

"What?"

"The man who proved and applied co-location… they'll remember him all right."

And all of a sudden it made sense — that was what this man, no, this *creature* wanted from me: co-location. It wanted a technology that would let it fold together two distant points in space, merging them into a single location, without the need for traversable wormholes and all the hazards and tradeoffs that go with them.

I thought of what this creature might achieve with such power, and my guts sank through my feet.

"I don't know what you're talking about."

Something changed in the air within that passageway, and for a split second, out of the corner of my eye, the bulkheads behind and to either side of him seemed to shift and warp. For a moment I thought I could hear breathing other than mine and his, the panting of some large and terrible things, unseen but no less substantial for it. Something was telling my brain that there was another presence in the passageway, and while I could not smell anything I wondered if I might be associating some unconsciously registered pheromone with a threat similar to the one Mol Gai had detected previously.

Stranger things had happened lately.

"You've spoken to her about co-location far, far too often to imagine that I'm going to fall for that," he said. "So maybe we can just be honest with each other. I need that technology, and that means I need *you*, and although I would much rather you weren't damaged it's not a strict requirement."

I took a step backwards, trying to see without seeing, and moved my head to sweep my peripheral vision across the passageway. Large areas of the bulkhead behind him seemed to warp as they left my field of vision, one, two, three patches of uncertainty, each of them maybe two to three meters across. I felt dark eyes upon me.

"I've come a long, long way to find you, Rex," he said. "Don't disappoint me now."

8

I ran and I ran and I ran. Mournful shrieks and wailing cries echoed throughout the passageways of the whole deck, and I am sure I heard the thundering of many heavy feet, the gallop of unknowable horrors racing after me. I slid down a ladder to the deck below, turned three corners then did the same thing again, ever terrified that I might bump into another crew member, another appendage of the multi-farious creature that sought to claim me for its own.

The truth I now understood was that *Ardent* was nothing to Him but a shiny bauble, a bonus prize. What He really wanted was *me*. The information I contained, the ways I could be weaponised… the possibilities were frightening.

And — oh my worlds — *co-location*. He knew what it was, and He wanted it so badly it had brought Him out into the great dark to capture me Himself, while I was far from any hope of intervention or rescue.

Imagine how far that *thing* could spread, with the knowledge of co-location in its possession.

I knew I would have to wipe out this cell, in case it had not known for sure I was aboard *Ardent* before taking over. I had to prevent the knowledge of what happened out here from getting back to the rest of the collective mind. He had to be made to think me dead, or missing, or otherwise unattainable. He had to stop looking for me. The extent of the abilities He would gain if He were to absorb me into His whole, and with me the knowledge of co-location, is difficult to judge. It is likely, however, that even at the least ambitious levels of utilisation His power would grow tenfold.

I had to stop that from happening, at any cost. On no account could this entity learn the equations and conditions and mechanisms that make co-location possible — such an outcome would cause the end of self-determination for all thinking species, in our galaxy and perhaps beyond it.

No, certainly beyond it. With a sufficiently powerful energy source there are no practical limits to how far one can travel, once one has mastered co-location technology.

I coursed through the plans of the ship, the schematics, the specifications. I raced and raged in swiftly computed visualisations of blueprints, strings of protocols written in free-floating nets of words, numbers, symbols, sliding and wrapping, folding around each other, a mental holo so intricate and complex, flowing with a compact sort of grace. I sought a way to make this ship into a weapon of my own, and while many options surfaced which I had not yet considered, for the sake of expediency I kept coming back to the all-hatch release plan.

On this deck there were also shouts and screams. Rounding a corner too quickly I was forced to leap over a crew member who was being dragged across the deck by two men in infantry fatigues. She called out to me, but I didn't stop.

You can't stop, I told myself. *There's too much at stake.*

As I moved I thought about how I could do what I needed to do swiftly, with no wasted seconds. I had a good idea how to launch and control a drone — that part was actually surprisingly easy. I had found the information the ship would expect to receive from a dry dock, and it would take me mere moments to discover whether I could access and copy that data from a drone control station, or whether I'd have to type it all in from memory. If the latter it would add about a minute to the total time.

I figured I could get this step done in a few short minutes, provided I did not make myself move so quickly that I made dumb mistakes. But that chance I might fail was significant, and carried with it significant consequences. I needed a backup plan.

I clicked my link.

"Zana Turei," I said. After a moment my link blipped. "Zana. Are you still… you?"

There was a very long moment before I got any reply.

"Only just. I think yes, I am."

"Good, I'm so very glad. I need your help, if you're still able?"

"I'll do what I can, Rex. What do you n—"

The link cut out mid-word, and try as I might I could not reconnect to Zana. My own holo and link were working perfectly fine, but hers would not receive. I tried calling through to work stations in the engineering section, but they too refused to allow a connection. She had been walled off from me, and I knew that had been done deliberately.

But she was still there, and still *her*, which was comforting to know.

Without the backup plan I would just have to make sure I didn't fail. I carried on, heading towards the launch bay, doing my best to avoid opening any hatches that might tell the bridge someone was moving about down here.

Light strips and illuminated panels began to go out, only the passageways were not quite the same as the maintenance shafts. Everywhere that crew were expected to function within the ship there were emergency lighting facilities which could not be shut off manually, and now stark, blue-white light emanated from the status strips near the overhead, lending everything around me an eerie, other-worldly glow.

Miraculously I arrived at the launch bay safe and sound. I

had no choice of course but to open the hatches to gain access, and once inside I found many doors of varying size and specification barring the entrance of basically every thoroughfare and cabin in the hangar command complex. Only two of these separated me from the control centre, and I wasted no time getting through them — from the moment I had opened that first hatch I had likely announced my presence here to everyone on the command deck, so now I focused on speed rather than stealth.

The control centre would have been very interesting, under different circumstances. The systems were of course holo-based, all in a low power state but still visible to the naked eye as broad swathes of dim light. A wide set of gallery-style windows gave a view onto the flight deck, where fighters and bombers were arrayed in storage. To each side of the landing pads, separated off by gantries and panelling, rows of cartridge-style racks held hundreds of combat drones in vertical storage positions.

I resumed the control system holos until I found the one which looked like it was intended for drone access. A quick check of everything drone-related I had committed to memory, and I was initiating the system.

What would have been convenient is if I could have simply interfaced my implant with the control system, and programmed in directives by imagining what I wanted to do. But no such luck — my particular augmentation has only a simple transceiver, most of which is actually security circuits, allowing it to request and obtain firmware updates without the risk of being compromised. In fact as far as I am aware, wireless brain–machine interfaces are pretty much illegal in the civilian sector. This, the first time I had wished I had access to such technology, was with the express wish that I might gain control of a drone with which to effect the murder of everyone aboard an Imperial Combine cruiser. And I am generally considered to be a moral and rational person, so perhaps that legal stance is very sensible and completely justified.

Much as I had expected — but still disappointing — the drone control system was fire-walled off from everything else. I could not simply copy across the information I wanted a drone to transmit on behalf of a fictional dry dock facility. It took me well over a minute to type out the relevant code segments and drag them across to the glyph for the first drone in the racks. After a moment's thought, I selected another group of drones and stacked them with instructions of their own. They could serve as a distraction to buy more time for my star player.

I brought up the first drone's navigation system and gave it new directives, telling it that it had to remain within a meter of the cruiser's hull. I ordered it to move to a holding position near the main antenna array and await a specific set of conditions. I had no intention of telling it to transmit its message until I was good and ready and safe, since knowing my luck I would otherwise have blown myself into space along with everyone else. No, the drone could wait until my criteria were met.

Up until that moment I don't think any of what I was planning had really seemed real. Yes, I had thought about the possibility of my life pod bumping into bodies as it streaked away from the ship, and the expressions that would be on people's faces as they were blown out into the airless cold of deep space. Even those of them who were in the thrall of the intruders aboard the ship would doubtless have involuntary reactions, their faces hard-wired to convey horror and terror while bleeding out precious air in futile screams. All of that though had seemed sort of hypothetical earlier on, as though it was merely a thought experiment I had been running. Now it was far more real.

My hands hovered over the controls.

But they were all enthralled, surely. All of them turned. I hoped to the many worlds of mankind I was right about that.

Zana wasn't turned just yet, I imagined. She would take longer to go, as would I, and ultimately she would still die with all the rest of them. But save her somehow and she would still become like the others. Then what? She might get the ship back under His control, that's what. She had to die with the crew, and she would have been the first to tell me that herself.

I executed my commands.

Orange warning lamps began to rotate in the launch bay below. The cartridge to the left of my view from the gallery window shunted forwards, and the whole rack containing the first array of drones folded outwards until it was married up with launch corridors built into the deck below. The drones disappeared into the chutes beneath them, which were then each closed off by a pair of sliding hatches.

A klaxon honked, and without warning everything in the bay outside the gallery windows powered down. The holos in front of me blinked out of existence. I'd been found out, and by now I knew the routine well enough. It was time to get moving again.

I walked briskly from the launch bay, heading aft again and keeping close to the bulkheads as I moved swiftly but silently down passageways. This time I was not careless enough to run, at least not until the first blood-curdling scream that sounded way too close. I climbed a ladder hurriedly between two decks, avoiding the elevators since they would undoubtedly be under surveillance.

What I needed now was access to the sensors — firstly to see if my drones had been launched successfully before power to the flight deck was killed off, and then secondly to knock out those same sensors so that my little life pod could escape the ship undetected.

I sneaked from place to place, managing somehow to remain unseen as once-people chased after still-people, but everywhere I went the holos and control stations were unresponsive. There was only one place I would be getting access to priority systems, other than the command deck. Zana had told me not to try to help her but there was now no other choice. Despite the risk it was something I simply had to do. I crept towards engineering like a thief going back for more.

The maintenance shaft at the rear of the engineering section was still unlocked and still unguarded, and I took this to be a good sign. If Zana had come under the full control of that organism already — if it knew what she knew — then it might have closed off this avenue I had into the heart of the ship. But then it could also have lain a trap, with the part I was meant to spring waiting for me behind the inner hatch.

It was with extreme caution that I opened the hatch into the main engineering compartment, but no traps were sprung. I saw nobody about — not the soldiers who had earlier solidified the presence of the creature who claimed to be called Voice, and not any of the usual engineering staff. A pair of booted feet and corresponding ankles was laid on the floor nearby, disappearing out of view behind a control station, and belonging to what I assumed was someone who had fallen and never got up again. I did my best not to look too closely as I exited the maintenance shaft. Part of me just did not want to know what had happened.

I stole my way through engineering, creeping slowly and quietly past the only operations alcove that appeared to be in use, staffed by solemn, silent engineers, and then I sneaked into the short passageway connecting Zana's office to main engineering. I tapped on the hatch as loudly as I dared while not being so quiet that she would not hear me from within.

"Zana, are you there? Zana let me in."

As it had been when I tried to talk to her last by link, there was a long wait before she answered.

"I can't Rex, I can't."

"Worlds, Zana! Let me in."

There was another long pause, then what might have been a muffled sob.

"I'm struggling to stay *me* right now. I don't trust what I'll do if you come in here and start meddling in the world that is made."

I closed my eyes. She was starting to sound less like herself, and more like someone under the influence of a megalomaniacal cult leader.

"Zana, please," I said. "Try to keep a grip on who you are. You're the chief snipe. You like to look after the tourists, if they're geeky enough. You're the one who *thinks* during conversations, and doesn't follow rules that don't need following — nobody tells you what to say and nobody tells you what to do. Please, *please*, just be Zana Turei."

There was another long silence, then the soft *hiss* of the seal releasing. The hatch opened slowly.

I pushed the hatch the rest of the way and entered the compartment. Inside the lighting was dim, and the whole place was incredibly messy, but I was mostly concerned with Zana. She had removed her work tunic and was wearing a vest with the lower half of her fatigues. Sweat stood out on her brow, and her hair draped in lank clumps. She was not at her best.

"Oh Zana," I said. I had no idea how to end that sentence. "You look… awful."

"Thanks," she said. "I feel awful."

"I need your help, while you're still you. Are you willing and able?"

"No guarantees I'm afraid. I can feel myself slipping away from… myself, I guess."

"I probably don't have much time here. He's after me."

"He's after all of us. I hear Him now, and the rest of the song is with Him. Beautiful."

"Well… yeah. Exactly. Listen, I launched a bunch of drones to help me deal with the ship, but someone interfered remotely. I need to know if those drones are carrying out their last instruction set. The launch bay controls are now dead, and nothing else lets me see tactical status."

"You came to the right place, civvy," she said. The timbre

of her voice made it sound like she was performing an induction speech for a set of new recruits. "Wait, let me try and remember how to do this."

Zana wobbled towards the holo display dominating one end of her office, and I took her arm gently and helped her across to it. Her skin felt freezing cold, yet it was clammy with sweat.

She swiped and tapped for a few seconds, and I saw from the display exactly what had happened before she even started reporting the results to me. My heart sank.

"All adrift," she said. "Poor lost drones."

She had found a view from the external sensors which showed the drones I had ejected, each of them receding gradually from the outer hull of *Ardent*, carried away by the momentum they had acquired as they exited their launch tubes. They all looked inactive, unpowered.

"They've been shut down?" I said.

"Seems that way, lil' pollywog. Have to stay here with us I guess."

Zana smiled at me in a way that was part blissful, part triumphant.

"As much as I'd like to, I really don't think that's workable," I said. "Zana, look at me. Try to remember who I am, what you think of me. Remember what we need to do."

My brain, or perhaps my implant, chose that moment to replay the memory of Zana telling me not to try anything heroic, and not to fall prey to the idiot notion that I might remind her of who she was and what her priorities were by appealing to her feelings about our short and ill-defined relationship. I have to admit I cringed a little.

"Rex," she said. My heart soared as high as it dared, which was not so terribly high. "Rex, I think I really am going."

She sobbed, and I held her for a moment. With my arms around her I could feel that her whole body was actually shaking a little.

"Strike back at Him," I said. "Put that creature on jankers like no-one has been janked before."

She pulled away suddenly, her body stiffening somewhat instead of leaning limply into me.

"Fuck Him," she said, "and fuck His song."

"That's the spirit," I said. "That's the Zana I know."

"He's going to win," she said. She looked me straight in the eye, as if determined I would entertain no foolish hopes on her behalf. "He will take me, it's only a matter of time. So you need a plan that can't be undone. Something that He won't be able to stop just because He finds out about it all of a sudden."

I scanned again through all the protocols and emergency procedures I had stored in memory, checking twice in the list of rejected ideas, but it took the chief snipe to pick one out for me.

"I have just the thing for this situation," Zana croaked. "What do you usually do with a virus?"

"Not sure what you mean," I said.

"Oh come *on*, I'm literally sweating it out all over you."

"Hit it... with a fever?"

"Exactly. Burn the fucker out."

"How the hell do we do that?"

Zana laughed drily and then coughed. I found her a hydration pack, removed the cap, and gave it to her.

"Sabotage protest fantasies, remember? Goes with snipe territory."

"Tell me what to do."

"Building a machine this complex, always going to be trade-offs even if it's spoken about as the most advanced thing we can manufacture. I can think of a good half-dozen little systems you could alter that would stop this thing dead."

"That's a great start," I said, "but you've seen that thing out there. I think you understand what it is, like I do. So I was hoping for something a bit more terminal."

Zana looked me straight in the eye again.

"Done more than see it. I can hear Him. Yes, you're right — I do understand."

"Help me to stop Him."

"One single component," she said. "Well, five instances of the same part. It's so critical there need to be redundancies."

"Yes, what'll happen if I take it?"

"People think life support is all about heating the ship," she said. "But it's not. The hull radiates heat far slower than the reactors generate it. Life support is about *cooling* the ship."

My mind focused in on the relevant sections of technical designs and emergency protocols.

"You're thinking about sabotaging heat dissipation."

"Yes. Kill the brains of the routing system between reactor coolant control and the thermal dissipation network. Only one of two things can then happen, no matter what steps the crew take — either the ship gets hotter and hotter until all organic life denatures, or energy builds up in the cores until they detonate. Either way, you'll have plenty of time to get away from here."

I wondered how it was I hadn't seen this particular strategy before. It was somewhat obscure, I supposed, and there would be no practical reason to call attention to it in general engineering procedures. And of course having access to the information was one thing; knowing how to use it with the experience of a lifelong engineer was a different thing altogether.

"I'm finding the schematics and access points now," I said. "Will you be able to make sure I can get access? Hatches might not be too reliable for me from here on in."

"From here, yeah. I'll keep an eye on you. Any hatches lock you out, I should be able to override them. Make you a path too."

"And shut down any polybots?"

"Piece of cake. And I have an idea for taking care of the

fighter bays and shuttle hangars — don't want anyone coming after you in one of those."

"What about the sensors outside? Can you hit them with a maintenance cycle as I launch my pod?"

Zana looked at me reproachfully, and rubbed her forehead.

"I don't know if I will last that long, but I will try. If you can find a backup plan for that one I'd make sure you're using that too."

I held her gently by the shoulders.

"I have every faith in the resolve and the abilities of my favourite Shadowback."

She smiled wanly.

"Speaking of sensors," I said, "He brought something aboard with him. I'm sure of it. I think it's what Mol Gai sensed in the passageways. Some kind of creature we can't see. Any chance a thing like that would show up on internal security?"

She tapped into the security interface of her holo and scanned the ship several times. Four different overlays failed to show anything unusual.

"Nothing," she said. "Any idea what I should be looking for?"

"Not a clue," I said. "No idea what they were, or how to find them."

"I'd say arm yourself, but I'm afraid none of the firearms we have around here will work for you. Bridge has control of the trigger suppression system, and even if I found a way around that you'd need a weapon you were authorised to fire. Which is none of them."

"You got a wrench?" I said. "Guess I'll take a big, heavy wrench."

"Have I got a wrench? I'm a Deep-damned engineer, Rex."

She pointed into a corner, where no fewer than three wrenches were propped up against the bulkhead. I picked up the largest one, and she laughed. Then she coughed. The coughing turned into a fit of gasping and croaking, and I handed her the hydration pouch again.

"You'd best get going," she said, after taking a few mouthfuls. "I don't know if I can hold on for much longer."

"I wish we'd had more time," I said. I hugged her. "I wish we'd found a better use for the time we did have."

"No point worrying about that now," said Zana. "Not going to bring myself down just to then have to—"

"—bring yourself up again?" I said.

"Exactly," she said.

I kissed her on the forehead, we touched our temples together, and she held me for a long moment, with one hand resting on my hip and the other at the back of my neck.

I'm no expert, but I think we both knew, before I left, what could have been.

9

———

I don't know how she managed to stay conscious and focused, but Zana Turei was the ally I wished I had had my whole life.

Hatches unlocked and opened ahead of me, charting a course through the engineering sections and carrying me forwards towards my goal. As I passed through each hatch I heard others opening and closing behind me, a false trail Zana was leaving for anyone trying to follow and predict my route from the command deck.

Twice on my way to the primary environmental control chamber I passed by inactive polybots. One was suspended in some kind of half-crawl, half-standing position, lurking around a corner like some great mantis ready to strike, and it made my heart leap into my mouth when I came across it. The other was less of a shock, frozen in place halfway emerged from a maintenance shaft and easy to spot from some distance along the passageway.

Zana was a guardian angel, that much was true for the moment.

By the time I reached environmental control a sheen of sweat was on my skin, and I was beginning to feel the cost of moving about in such quick and fearsome bursts, a type of activity to which I am in no way accustomed.

But I had plenty of energy left for wanton destruction.

Finding the coursing modules in the energy routing system was easy, and I was surprised at how few physical barriers stood between them and my heavy wrench. All I had to do was unlatch a circular plasteel cover from each module's cabinet, and there they were. They were each as large as my luggage, but easy enough to smash into literal pieces with a good, heavy wrench.

Red lamps flashed in every bulkhead from the moment the first module imploded, and I heard automatic valves closing somewhere within the inter-deck void spaces. A siren shrieked, and as soon as all five modules were destroyed — plus the six backup modules which were foolishly stored in the adjacent compartment — I was on my way again.

I headed for the aft lower decks, towards a cluster of escape pods which the deck plan in my head now centred on. I linked to Zana, not knowing whether she was listening or not, or whether the comms route to her link was still being blocked.

"Still with me?"

Her link stayed silent, refusing to talk back to mine, but the public address system clicked once.

"You might have a new problem. Stand by."

It was her voice, wobbly but determined, and despite the ominous message I smiled to myself. I rounded the next corner and came to a sudden halt, all the wind taken out of my sails. She told me what was happening even as I came across the results.

"He's ejecting life pods. I doubt He knows exactly what we're up to, but He's definitely trying to keep you here."

In front of me, the entire length of the concave bulkhead was marked off by regular indentations which would until quite recently have held single-occupant life pods. One per crevice, each of them capable of preserving a single life for a short time in even the direst of situations. Every crevice was empty, every pod gone.

"The pods on the decks above and below you are also missing," said Zana's voice. "Ahh, my *head*. Sorry. Okay, you need to get across to the outer port-side hull instead. One deck down though — someone is already there on this deck, and they're ejecting those pods too. Move it!"

I ran as though the hounds of hell were after me, which — given that I was unable to see and identify the creatures accompanying the man called Voice — I suppose could well have been happening.

I dropped down to the deck below, sliding down a ladder the same way I had seen crew members do it, and allowed myself to sink into a crouch as I landed, checking each way along the blue-lit passageway before moving off.

"Nearly there," said the disembodied voice of Zana Turei. "Careful, He probably knows where you are. But He has to eject the pods manually, so you still have time."

Her voice was shaky this time, and I imagined her struggling to keep control of it. I didn't reply — even if she could hear me, the chances were that someone was waiting nearby to ambush me. I saw no reason to give away my position.

I crept quickly but quietly along the passageway, heading for the escape pods for this side of the ship. They were so very close. So close. Closer… I had them in sight.

The gentle curve of the passageway brought the pods into view one by one, and it was not until I was a couple of meters away from the nearest pod that He swung into view.

"Leaving, are you?"

I froze. I looked to the sides, to my left and to my right, and in my peripheral vision I saw the slight movements of undefinable masses behind Him. He had brought His companions.

"You know how far I've come to find you," Voice said. "Like I said, I would prefer not to damage you."

"Stay back."

"Or what? Really, Rex. You won't be able to cycle a pod before I get to you. They're fast to activate, but not *that* fast."

"Stay where you are, I mean it. This ship is about to die, and I have no intention of staying."

"You have no leverage. But then you don't *need* leverage, Rex. You and I are leaving here together, and that's the end of it. Come with me, Rex. Come to the shuttle bay. Let's leave this doomed ship together, in peace and in safety."

He kept coming, stepping towards me slowly but steadily. The faint sounds of other creatures' breath came with Him.

"Hey," said Zana.

"What?" He looked around, then seemed to realise this new participant was talking over the address system. "Behave yourself, Zana Turei."

"You stay right where you are, big mouth, or you'll find it real fucking hard to find yourself a shuttle that's not molten slag."

I smiled to myself and slapped the large and obvious control next to the nearest escape pod. Its canopy popped open obligingly, and I hooked a leg inside.

"You can't interrupt the cycle that's started," I said. "It will continue to feed itself cumulatively, and if you do manage to break that cycle somehow then the reactors will explode anyway."

His insincere smile continued, but somehow it now seemed less like he really meant it. Shadows played across the curved bulkheads of the passageway behind him, and people began running frantically into the escape pod chamber. They got as close as he was, then stopped dead, panting and staring at me with grotesquely wide eyes. Ouellet was in amongst them, and Mister Cona, and poor al-Rashid, and others I had seen here and there. Scientists from the briefing, soldiers from the infantry detachment, men and women from all across the ship. But without any obvious command or gesture from Him, they stayed their feet and hands obediently.

"You can choose to die in a slow fire, or a fast one," I said. "That is your last meaningful choice aboard the *Ardent*. I am leaving."

"With me," he said. "In a shuttle."

"He's not going anywhere with you," said Zana.

I heard a snarl come from somewhere across the compartment, and Voice took another step towards me. The throng behind him also took a step forward, moving in unison. Something indiscernible rippled visibly from deck to bulkhead to overhead, sweeping past him and surging my way.

"No more warnings, fucker!" Shouted Zana.

A booming, crashing sound reverberated through the passageways, and I realised that I was hearing an explosion somewhere forward of us. The rippling pattern froze against the overhead, and a petulant sound whimpered down from it.

"That was the auxiliary shuttle bay," said Zana. "You or your pals take one more step between you, and all the bays go. And yes, I *can* see those ugly motherfuckers you've brought with you."

I don't know what she was doing to the bays — perhaps she had found some way to detonate ordnance by remote — but in that moment I could sense a Zana Turei bluff in her words. She almost certainly couldn't see the creatures with Voice. I hoped to all the many worlds of mankind that he didn't know that.

"Sensors are down, Rex. Now's your moment."

I hooked my other leg into the pod, and then settled my butt into it.

"You'll never find me out there," I said. "By the time you have the sensors fixed, my tiny pocket of life will be beyond the most granular resolution of which they are capable. I will sail on into the dark, forever beyond your grasp. I might never be found. If that means I die, so be it."

Voice lunged towards me and spat—

"Then you *die!*"

At some level I must have known my hand had never

been empty, and purely out of instinct I swung the wrench as hard as I possibly could. Voice's face collapsed in on itself immediately, and unfortunately I got a very clear view of that happening before the borrowed human body crumpled to the deck beside my pod. That memory will last.

I hit the most prominent control inside the pod and its opaque canopy began to slam down immediately. It was extremely quick to close, and the release mechanism for the pod itself was juddering even before the canopy had sealed shut. I just had time to hear a chain of explosions off in the distance as something heavy slammed into my pod and a sound like claws on steel rang painfully loud in my ears, blotting out everything else.

Something went *BRUNK* behind me, and then I felt like I was hurtling feet first down a covered slide.

I think that just about brings us up to the current moment.

Yes. That is the story of how I came to be where I am now, rocketing no doubt to my doom. I can't imagine anyone will ever recover this data, but since I will eventually drift into what is currently human-occupied territory, and a million solars hence it may still be populated by whatever it is our species becomes, I suppose I do have to consider the probability of my being discovered to have a non-zero value. I wouldn't want to claim an absolute, after all.

My prospects, though, are not what you would call 'good'.

Escape pods like this one are not supposed to be used for ranged transport, or even for long-term survival. They're expected to keep a single individual alive only for the few hours it would normally take Life and Rescue's emergency craft to arrive alongside a ship that is no longer habitable. At the limits of their provisioning, such pods will keep someone alive for a few days, no more, and the mental state of the occupant at the end of that period is something about which I doubt the manufacturer makes any warranties. The usable space in here is not much larger than I am, the air cycling unit will certainly have its limitations, and having explored every sliding storage recess I have found the rations to be minimalist, to say the least.

There is also nothing to do. No holo screen, no viewport, nothing to occupy the mind but a three-diagram hatch ejection procedure, stencilled in orange, white, and red, right in front of my face. It is neither complicated nor entertaining.

I can only really look inwards.

While I recline mandatorily in near-silence, unable to witness the trillion-fold treasures of the yawning gulf through which I slip unobserved, I review the great mass of data I have accumulated since the beginning of this strange and unfortunate voyage. I tie the loose threads, unburden myself of the useless information and conversational dead ends, reorganise the temporal backbone of the memories, and add a few narrative threads capable of being comprehensible to a third party. I review my memories over and over, cross checking what I think I experienced against the checksum data provided by my implant, desperate to ensure that no incongruities exist, hoping I will finish this mammoth task before my brain is harmed irreparably by a lack of oxygen, a surplus of carbon dioxide, or — an outside chance, but one which occupies a justifiably large corner of my mind — terminal impact with some unknowable and indifferent heavenly body.

It all needs to be just right. This is, after all, to be not only my personal journal of these final experiences, but my log of events aboard the *Ardent*, preserved faithfully for the elucidation of those who might come later. A black box data recorder, if you will. I wonder if anyone has ever constructed a record of events from such a source before. I wonder if they called it a red box data recorder.

In amongst my deliberate editing and diligent curating, I have unlimited time to think.

I think of al-Rashid and his fine new ship, sailing out into the black with all the best wishes of the admiralty carrying him forth on a wave of hope.

I think of the other scientists and engineers who set out with me, each of them brilliant, each of them so willing to help the navy. Each of them expecting to return home with their own pocketful of stars.

I think of Mol Gai, a kindred spirit from another species, descended from the soils of his home world in a more fundamental way than I or indeed any other human is descended from the earth, yet possessed of such a familiar yearning, that same urge to reach out to any *elsewhere* still unvisited; a creature whose life deserved from the universe a far, far better culmination than the brutal act with which his final moment was wrought upon him.

I think of Zana. Smart, beautiful, kind, and funny. Compassionate and understanding. All qualities one would opt to include in the theoretical and wishful imaginary construct standing in for a person to whom one is attracted, but also — and I have verified the memories a dozen times over — qualities that were well-evidenced by her authentic matching of words to deeds.

She, the first of them all to pass my litmus test for a worthy soul, a soul who until she came into my world had been so largely hypothetical, and a litmus test which, until Zana, might as well have been an impassable barrier.

She, who had shown me that the reason it takes a lifetime to meet a person capable of fulfilling an ideal is because it is only at the moment of that meeting one realises a lifetime *had to pass* before that moment could possibly occur; that it is only in arriving with surprise at such a destination — only in the ending of one journey — that the true nature of what has passed becomes visible; that it is that moment which *frames* the prior experience, and *marks* the previous epoch, and prompts one to pause and say 'look you now, look on here behind me, look upon the days that are past. All that you look upon was a lifetime in and of itself, and I define it so because it holds within it all of, and only, the days and years in which *you* were not yet there beside me.'

She, who returned me to being who I am, by killing who I was, allowing me to kill him and replace him, allowing me to become myself, to begin a new journey, to create the grand new epoch of lifetime yet to be.

This is the way it is. Of course, of course. Always and everywhere, the lifetimes are bookmarked by the rise and call of a singular form of recognition, of belonging, and then of endings and beginnings. I think…

I think the air in here must be getting thin already.

I feel my heart thumping in my chest. The pain behind my eyes has become a searing sheet. And yet, despite the conditions, these might be the truest thoughts I have ever had. It is most unfortunate that I am light years from anyone, and surely destined to experience what is likely to be — statistically speaking — the most lonely demise in the entire human story.

Sometimes I really hate this Deep-damned, bastard universe.

Strange thoughts rise like spectres beneath a veil, melt away before I can focus on them. The headache is worsening.

I think.

I structure and edit and optimise memories. I think. I draw water from a hydration pack, which grows ever more worryingly flaccid. I think. I worry, though it is needless since everything — literally everything — is now beyond my control. I think. I nibble on a ration stick, and imagine that its formulator must have been bored and resentful in their role. I think.

Sometimes I jerk awake from a drifting state, a spasm of jumbled consciousness in which the manifold anxieties of my situation — both in the present and the recent past — force me so very hard to flee from unseen monsters that my body, prepared as it is to rest in sleep, has no option but to lash out against, repelling their savagery no matter how uncoordinated its supposed counter-attack may be.

I think. And therefore, I suppose, *I am.*

I really feel in this moment, more so than I ever have before, that that is very important. I feel the urge to sing it at the top of my lungs, and the harmony with which to do so is within me already. I cannot for the life of me imagine why.

I think.

I try to rest, to quiet my mind and accept my situation. It is for the most part futile. I try to sleep, to lower my heart rate and the depth of my breath. Every second gained from the life support means the slightest increase to my chances, no matter how fractional. Most of the time I am not successful. The moments without consciousness are few and far between, and when they do come they are mostly fitful and surreal, spiralling me back to conscious thought on the crests of chaotic white waves.

I am.

When I *do* sleep, sometimes, on those few occasions when I slip away from myself for long enough to sink down, down deep, far below the anxieties which quite expectedly plague me now, far below the reach of monsters, sometimes I am fortunate, and in those sorely precious engulfments, longing to survive but willing never to awaken, sometimes, I dream of Damastion.

THE END

Also read the optional short novel:
A Storm to the Savage.

This series of main sequence novels ends now, with
Whom Gods Shall Fear, Part One,
available already, and concluding soon in…
Whom Gods Shall Fear, Part Two.

ABOUT THE AUTHOR

R. Curtis Venture was born in the United Kingdom in the late Seventies. His first great passion was for science fiction, both in books and on the screen, and he spent his childhood years imagining other worlds. Originally a graduate of Applied Biology, he is — through an unlikely but plausible series of circumstances — now employed full-time in the legal sector.

When not consumed with a creative binge, his free time is mostly spent hiking up mountains and through forests, camping in the wilderness, reading widely, or working towards the current milestone of 2,000 films watched.

Why not visit him at his author website? As well as short stories and articles about the Armadaverse, self-publishing, and the craft of writing, it includes posts about bushcraft, wild-camping, and the great outdoors: outdoorsauthor.blog

CONNECT AND EXPAND!

Scan the QR code below to learn more about this series of Armada Wars!

Visit the official site for:
The cheapest paperback prices, signed editions of new releases, news, in-universe lore, exclusive merchandise, and of course the official newsletter:
ArmadaWars.com

www.ingramcontent.com/pod-product-compliance
Lightning Source LLC
Chambersburg PA
CBHW021955170726

47994CB00021B/507